DEAT[illegible]
VARIATIONS

Ivon Baker

KEYHOLE CRIME
London · Sydney

First published in Great Britain 1977
by Robert Hale Ltd.

This edition published 1981 by
Keyhole Crime, 15–16 Brook's Mews,
London W1A 1DR

ISBN 0 263 73682 2

The characters and situations in this book are entirely imaginary and bear no relation to any real person or actual happening.

Set in 10 on 10 point Times Roman

Photoset by Rowland Phototypesetting Ltd.,
Bury St Edmunds, Suffolk
Made and printed in Great Britain by
Cox & Wyman Ltd., Reading.

CHAPTER ONE

NOON. Monday July 12—Bicentennial Year. At the Mobil service station south of Pittsfield an attendant sponged my fly-spattered windshield and directed me across the web of minor roads around Lenox. I was among the Berkshires for the first time, yet already those wooded hills were familiar from Anne's home movies taken on vacation at her father's summer place near Tanglewood. That was just up the road and if Stanley Dowland was in residence I might encounter his bronzed Bentley at any turn. My wife's father is a good friend—reason enough we should not meet, that blazing day.

Ten minutes driving—an imposing stone arch loomed on my right. FOXDALE ACADEMY—dedicated by its century-old charter to the enlightenment and education of the daughters of gentlepeople. I swung off the road to find my way barred by massive iron gates.

Enter, stage left, one hollow-chested retainer loosely draped in uniform worthy of the Ruritanian Militia. He stooped to my level and breathed mint-laden miasma from between ruminant jaws.

'*Yup?*' The challenge was leisured . . . the jaws ceased not to gyrate.

My ID wallet impressed him. 'You expected, Colonel Barrington, sir?'

I nodded.

'Have to check that, sir.' He was away to a phone beside the gate. Sixty seconds I sweltered . . . then the gates swung and he was waving me on like a matador passing the bull beneath his cape.

Onto a cool serpentine drive flanked by long-spent rhododendrons—their dark green dappled by heady sun. Another quarter mile and the shrubbery opened to sweeping lawns and a stone facade in English Jacobean style. I pulled up by a flight of wide steps and climbed stiffly from the car. A long drive from Boston.

'Colonel Barrington?' A stern woman with greying hair. 'I'm Fiona Harkness.' The name meant nothing but the aura of authority suggested top academic brass. We shook hands. 'Clare is getting herself ready. You've chosen a marvellous day for a picnic. I'm sure she'll enjoy it all the more for its being so unexpected. Her father called less than an hour ago. Of course, we have to be just a *little* bit strict about—what shall I say?—*unscheduled* visits.' A wintry smile. 'But this is one occasion when I'm happy to make an exception. Most of the girls have been home for the celebrations . . . but the Senator is so *very* busy these days. I'm afraid Clare hasn't seen much of him, this year. Ah—and here's the young lady herself.'

Clare Patterson—just two months past her fifteenth birthday. Blue check shirt and faded jeans emphasized her boyish figure as she hurried across the entrance hall. Fiona Harkness surveyed her charge with a bleak professional smile. I sensed private disapproval of informal dress to which she was compelled to give public sanction. The Harkness features were eloquent. They had already contradicted her expressed pleasure at my visit.

Clare snatched my hands impulsively. 'Uncle George!' Behind severe thick-rimmed glasses her brown eyes were alight with excitement. Standing on tiptoe she kissed my cheek. 'Who's looking after the Pentagon?'

I ruffled her hair. 'An inflatable replica behind my desk. Nobody will notice the difference. You're looking well, young woman. How's the music coming along?'

A glow of genuine pleasure from Fiona Harkness. 'We're very pleased with her, Colonel. Of course, you'll know she's playing in the inter-state festival at Tanglewood. However, I've had to remind her that ability as a violinist is complementary to academic achievement and no substitute for it.' She turned to Clare. 'Run along and enjoy yourself, my dear. I know Colonel Barrington has only a short time—and I'm sure it's very good of him to come out of his way to see you.'

In the car the girl said, 'How did I do?'

I smiled. 'Convincing. Made me feel about ninety.'

Acknowledging the creaky salute of the Ruritanian Militiaman, I turned right, towards the Berkshire Section of Highway 90 and Albany, thirty miles distant.

Clare said, 'Who are you?'

Good question. She had never seen me before. I recalled the words of my Director, spoken on the Boston waterfront four hours earlier. '*The abduction of a female minor is viewed with disfavour alike by Senate and People in these United States.*' That thought had hounded me west along Highway 90. He had stood there, looking out of place as a turkey on a Manhattan sidewalk, his bulky form blocking my view of *Britannia* making ready for sea. '*The abduction of a female minor . . .*' His way of saying if things went wrong I would look in vain for a glimpse of him in court. I had watched him board the harbour launch and head out across choppy water, bound for a leisurely cruise to Nova Scotia in exalted company. Contrast that with the rented Ford in which I crossed Massachusetts and you have the story of my life. He set up the hoops—I jumped.

Turning to the girl I spoke naturally for the first time since leaving Boston. 'David Meynell—Ministry of Defence, London.'

'You're British?'

'*English.* A subtle distinction but one I cherish. How much did your father tell you?'

She stared ahead. 'That there was trouble. That you'd be a friend and I was to trust you.'

'And treat me like Uncle George?'

She smiled. 'That was acting. Uncle George Barrington is a stuffed shirt. Now he *is* about ninety. Always has been. I'd trade you for him any day. Where are we going?'

'Albany Airport.'

We touched down at Montreal early that evening and took a cab across the St Lawrence to the RCAF field east of Jacques Cartier. Above the 49th Parallel bicentennial fever had given place to pre-Olympic symptoms. Security was tight—typical of the edginess surrounding international games since Munich. At the camp gate we left the cab and hurried through rods of rain to a waiting Air Force bus. Ten minutes later we were aboard a cumbersome jet transport, elbowing its way through cloudbase towards a shrouded sunset. Cabin lights exaggerated the gloom beyond rain-streaked windows.

Above the clouds high summer returned. The fluffy horizon tilted as we swung on course. A white-jacketed steward brought laden trays—my first hot food since breakfast. I ate hungrily—and found life more tolerable. This enterprise was the province of athletic men who live out of suitcases and tote automatics as lesser mortals carry credit cards. By nature I am far from athletic, my work is largely sedentary and seldom involves contact with firearms.

Sixteen years before, I had recruited into DHR2—*Defence—Historical Research (Armed Services)*—a Department which worked from a grotty Edwardian office in the warren of Whitehall, venturing forth to examine military relics, post-1936 vintage. Mostly our findings were of academic interest—but there were others. Even after twenty or thirty years, a wrecked aircraft or a sunken sub may yield secrets highly embarrassing for people who think themselves safe from retribution. Occasionally I was summoned as expert witness for the prosecution. And there were times when retribution tarried not upon due process of law. Up to the Director's office would go the files. Down from that Olympian height they came to the sections—each olive-green cover embellished with ciphered instructions from the pen of that grey eminence in his panelled room. *NA*—no action to be taken at this juncture. *DPP*—prepare as evidence for the Director of Public Prosecutions. And *TCO* . . .

A century ago—that's how it seems now—he scrawled that cryptogram on one of my reports and invited me to see the job through to what proved a messy finale. *Invited.* Just to establish a precedent. *TCO*—Take Care Of. Past master in the craft of euphemism is our Director.

A bullet under my left shoulder-blade earned transfer to D19—*Defence Lands Conservation (Sites and Buildings)*. The Department exists to ensure protection for historic properties requisitioned by the armed services.

Mediaeval castles to Victorian hotels. With my transfer came the Director's personal and solemn promise of non-active service within the confines of the United Kingdom.

From which you will readily understand my fleeting presence in Western Massachusetts, masquerading as a senior officer of the United States Army.

Clare set down her plastic coffee cup and stared out at dazzling cloud sculpture. The RAF fit rear-facing seats in passenger compartments and she was looking directly into the setting sun. I saw her frown.

'East?' Her voice was puzzled.

'A long way.'

'Where *is* my father?'

I shrugged. 'Your guess is as good as mine. When he called you this morning he was in Kingston, Jamaica. Now—' I spread my hands.

'He's in danger?' Her eyes were troubled.

'Vulnerable. Right now he's where no representative of your administration should be—officially. There are times, in government, when your left hand mustn't know what your right hand is doing. It's a form of insurance. Your father's involved in very delicate negotiations—what his opponents would call back-door diplomacy. He succeeds—your government goes all coy and modestly claims another victory in the cause of detente. He fails—the whole enterprise is quietly swept under the carpet. Things go badly wrong—he's just another bleeding heart trying a Kissinger without authority or approval. And he's back lecturing on economics.'

She looked unhappy. 'I wish he was. Politics is dirty. What did you mean about being vulnerable? Because things might go wrong?'

'Because certain people are determined things *shall* go wrong. They believe all this talk of detente is window-dressing—a threat to western security.'

'Huh!' She tossed her head. 'A threat to vested interests.'

'That too. So your father has to fail—and you're his Achilles' heel. According to our information, you were to be snatched at your next Youth Orchestra rehearsal over at Tanglewood.'

'Tomorrow.'

'Which is why I arrived today.'

She sat silent for a while, then turned and peered at me over the rims of her glasses—a duchess appraising the new under-footman. 'But how do you fit into all this?'

'NATO,' I said darkly. It was near enough true.

She was only partly satisfied. 'You don't look one bit like an agent.'

'Thank God for that. I only do the job part-time. Mondays, Wednesdays and Fridays when there's an R in the month.'

She was growing drowsy. 'You're okay. Kind of . . . reassuring.' Her dark lashes drooped and she settled more comfortably into the seat.

Far away to the west piled clouds rose like a tinted iceberg from the dull grey waters of the Atlantic. I pulled a tired pack of cards from my pocket and settled to the soothing delights of Patience. My anodyne—and addictive. I can play for hours, game after game, my mind purged for inspiration.

As the transport crawled ponderously from the sun's setting towards its new arising I laid red on black, black on red—and thought of the interrupted work awaiting me. Archaeologist by profession and inclination, I had been commissioned to prepare a popular handbook of historic defence property now open to the public. For eighteen months I had researched and gathered material. April. The Director began to show signs of impatience. May. He set me an October deadline. June. He told me to take a month away from the uninspiring confines of Whitehall and work without interruption. But on Saturday July 10 I was hounded from my retreat in the midland shires and, at the behest of that same Director, whisked across to Boston for a hurried briefing in security staff quarters aboard *Britannia.* My protest that Johnson, Garbett or Masters could have done the job, received a typical reply.

'Dear boy, you have two unsurpassed qualifications for this assignment. Your features are utterly devoid of guile—and your charming wife was educated at Foxdale Academy.'

Only then did I learn that Anne and I were expected to act *in loco parentis* until Clare's father had completed his mission. Work without interruption!

Beside me, the girl slept soundly. The cards came out right three times in succession. I reached up and switched off the light above our heads.

I woke her when the call came to fasten safety-belts. The note of the engines changed and we felt initial hesitation as the aircraft descended the first step of a long stairway to touchdown. The sunbright starboard wing dipped, pulling a gentle green landscape into view.

She blinked and stared at the slow-moving panorama, assessing each new feature. As we moved in over the outer markers she turned a puzzled face to me.

'England,' I said.

Our wheels yelped on to the runway.

8 am BRITISH SUMMER TIME. TUESDAY JULY 13. The year of the drought.

CHAPTER TWO

A WRAF sergeant led me to a downstairs room in the HQ building where Ron Metcalfe opened one weary eye and waved feebly from the depths of a regulation-issue armchair.

'All serene, boyo?'

I nodded. Like the Director on that Boston waterfront, he seemed out of place. Ron's natural habitat is that same shabby office in Whitehall, ostensibly devoted to historical research. I have long doubted that he had any other home. There he would lurk, nervously sucking antacid Rennies and worrying about people like me. The sight of his troubled face had come to mean journey's end. Today was different. Our encounter at RAF Finningley—two hundred miles north of London—marked only a brief hiatus in an unfinished exercise.

He yawned. 'You look the way I feel—squalid. Where's the girl?'

'Freshening up—and trying to adjust to being here. She'd got it we were heading for Jamaica. Not exactly delighted with her destination.'

'Huh!' He sat up. 'Like it or lump it. If she gets stroppy, mate, just remind her where she could have ended up. How much does she know?' He unwrapped a Rennie and began to crunch it noisily.

'I've told her *why*. Now she knows *where*. That's all.'

'It's enough. Now go smarten yourself up. You're a walking disaster-area.'

I ambled down the corridor to a washroom where the mirror confirmed Ron's strictures. Even my shaver protested. Ten minutes later I was back. As my hand grasped the doorknob I heard Ron's voice.

'. . . and Mrs Meynell's American, so you'll feel at home. As for the prof . . . calling himself a part-time agent is his daft idea of humour. Master of Arts, University of Oxford . . . head of a government department . . . Professor of Military History . . .' *Enough.* I opened the door. Ron regarded me critically. '. . . and a damn sight more presentable than he was ten minutes ago. So treat him with the respect he deserves.'

In another of the green-upholstered armchairs Clare sat clutching a fringed leather shoulder bag—the only luggage she could bring from Foxdale without exciting comment. For the first time I realised what a traumatic experience this could be for the girl—transported overnight into an alien environment. My homecoming would be another step into the unknown for her.

'We'll be living on a *boat*?' Her tone implied anything but delight at the prospect. 'I get seasick on the Manhattan ferry. Do we *have* to?'

I patted her arm. 'Wait and see.'

Ron drove us across country, skirting Doncaster to join the M1, then south through Nottinghamshire until we turned off the motorway below Derby. Then by narrow lanes and through drowsy villages we edged westwards to the lonely stretch of canal where our floating home was moored.

Plantagenet—fifty-six feet of black steel hull and green painted cabintop, built on traditional narrow-boat lines.

An idyllic homecoming. Bach's Sixth *Brandenburg* on

the hi-fi . . . tempting culinary smells drifting up from the galley . . . but best of all—Anne in shorts and tee-shirt, a warm smile of relief and welcome lighting her suntanned face as she shot up the companionway into my arms.

We ate. We talked. We relaxed—and tension eased from Clare's face. I did my best to explain why *Plantagenet* had been chosen as her refuge.

'Your father wants you out of America. He's up against a handful of ruthless men—but he's convinced they have contacts in every State of the Union. Ordinary decent folk with no interest in power or politics. Maybe he imagines things worse than they are—but I can't blame him for being over-cautious. Here in England the problems aren't over. There's still a chance you might be recognised.' I reached for a map of the British waterways system and spread it on the saloon table. 'The object of the exercise is to get off the map. How? By disappearing *into* the map. See all these coloured lines? *Canals*. They run the length and breadth of the country. Some broad, some narrow. *Plantagenet* is six feet ten wide. That means she can travel almost anywhere on that system. Looks impressive, doesn't it—but if you take an ordinary road map you won't notice the canals. We crossed this one five times on the way here—did you know that? No—and that's the way it is for most people. We're off their map.'

Ron crunched his tenth Rennie of the day. 'You hope. This is the Old Man's idea—and he's welcome to it.'

He was still morose when I saw him into his car. 'The old boy network, boyo. It sticks in my gullet. Patterson did us a favour when he was over here with the CIA. Ah—didn't know that, did you? Twenty years back—before your time. But that's not what this is all about. This is personal—the Old Man and one other. Patterson doesn't come into it. The Old Man hardly knows him and he certainly wouldn't stick his neck out like this to repay a twenty-year-old favour by a junior CIA agent. No—if you want my opinion—this whole operation was set up after a right royal dinner at the White House, last week. Top secret. Nothing in black and white. Nothing on tape.'

'I'd heard a whisper.'

'Uhuh—aboard *Britannia*. In the States nobody knows a damn thing. That puts us way out on a limb. If things come unstuck, there's going to be hell to pay. This top-level buddy-buddy routine is all very well, but it could cockup a first-class working relationship with US security. Professional ethics. Such things *do* exist, even in our line of business. Nobody likes to feel he hasn't the confidence of the man at the top—and nobody likes to be made a fool of. I tell you, boyo, I can smell trouble a-brewing.'

'Pessimist.'

'You reckon? Just pray I'm wrong. It's your neck. I'm damned if I see why the Department should be used—you especially. No offence, but this kind of caper isn't your scene. And how about Anne? She's wanted *out* ever since you stopped that bullet in Istanbul—and she hates the Old Man's guts. Oh yes. He crooks his finger . . . you come running—and she's worried sick. You saw how she was this morning.' He switched on the engine. 'And how much writing d'you think you'll do while you're playing Mary Poppins to that kid?'

* * *

We fixed Clare up in a guest cabin near the bows—a tiny closet eight feet by three and a half. *But now I am cabin'd, cribb'd, confin'd, bound in to saucy doubts and fears.* I hoped not—but the little cubicle was suddenly very like a prison cell.

A spell at the tiller of a narrow-boat shrinks life's problems to tolerable proportions. Beside me on the tiny after-deck, Anne leaned against the varnished safety-rail. She did not share the helmsman's euphoria.

'Ron's right. That fat old man dreamed up this plan without a thought of what it means to drag a girl halfway across the world. D'you realize that kid has nothing but the clothes she stands up in, two pairs of panties and a pajama top?'

I throttled back the thumping diesel and edged the tiller over to swing clear of an optimistic angler. 'Stop off at the next town we come to. One visit to Marks and Sparks should do the trick.' I took her hand and placed it on the tiller-arm. 'Take over while I check the map.'

Charts have no place among the navigational equipment of a traveller along England's canals. Maps and guidebooks ease his passage, depicting waterways as broad lines to which cling roads, railways and rivers. These attendant features form no link with the world beyond the towpath. If the mapmakers are to be believed, vast empty deserts begin half a mile from the liquid highways. The result is more than cartographical eccentricity—it is a way of life . . . a scheme of values speedily acquired.

Down in the after-cabin I studied the guidebook, running my finger along the broad blue line in search of a mooring for the night. Prolonged hot dry weather had brought water shortage and restrictions on the use of the canal—locks closed by early evening. I selected a site, then let my eye wander down the page to see what the morrow might bring.

Tongstone Priory. I had forgotten that it lay on our route—there in the meadows beside a canalized section of the River Wilde.

Back on deck I perched on the cabin top and watched Anne pilot *Plantagenet* across a narrow aqueduct.

'Remember Stephen Garland?'

She nodded, her eyes fixed on the course ahead. 'Beard. Grand gestures. Like Sir Walter Raleigh. Sure, I remember him. Called on us about two years back. Head of your old department at one time, wasn't he?'

'He recruited me. Brilliant man. Taught me a lot. I took over from him when he resigned.' I leaned back on the hot cabin roof, recalling those early days when I was new to the job—the long silent battlefields of Alamein and Tobruk . . . the Greek Islands . . . that perfectly-preserved Hudson bomber with its crew still aboard, frozen for twenty years in arctic ice . . .

'So?'

I sat up. 'Huh?'

'So what about Stephen Garland?'

'I've just noticed—we'll be passing his ancestral abode tomorrow. Think I'll stop by and consult him about my book.'

We devoured tea and slabs of fruitcake on deck, chugging slowly past tall factories where turbanned girls waved enviously from open windows. Our mooring for the night was below an isolated lock within earshot of the never-ending roar of motorway traffic. At dinner I talked about Stephen Garland.

'Born out of his time. Walter Raleigh? *Mmm.* Sir Philip Sidney. God knows why he joined the department. Brilliant mediaevalist—far better qualified than I—yet there he was, scratching about in North Africa for stuff less than forty years old. Waste of good talent. I've a sneaking suspicion the murkier side of our work appealed to him.' I leaned forward and spoke in a sepulchral whisper. *'The mad lust for adventure!'*

Anne tossed her head. 'Huh!'

'Family failing. His brother was a mercenary. Fight anyone if the pay was right. Not that Stephen was perfect. A ruthless streak. Not popular in the department. Got on with him all right, myself. We both treated the Civil Service as a joke.'

Clare said, 'I guess he'll be an old man by now.'

'Depends how you rate *old.* In his fifties, I'd say. Resigned ten years ago. Had his fill of excitement, I suppose.'

Anne nodded approvingly. 'Sensible man. And then settled down to farm the family acres. Something constructive for a change.'

Her tone was an unnecessary reminder that her father had written hinting that if I applied for the Chair of Classical History at Hampton University I might—as they say—hear something to my advantage. I believed him. Stanley Dowland was a governor and respected benefactor of that once-puritan college. Two good reasons why I was reluctant to accept his generous offer.

I woke in the pale light of dawn to find Anne gripping my shoulders as I writhed and struggled.

'It's all right, darling,' she murmured urgently. *'It's all right!'*

I put a hand to my forehead and felt sweat cold on the palm. The sound of my heart seemed to be thudding against walls and bulkheads in our tiny stateroom.

Months since I'd had a nightmare like that.

'Sorry.' My voice was thick, unrecognizable. 'Shouting again?'

'Trying to. Want to talk about it?' She put her arm round me and held my throbbing head against the warm smoothness of her breast.

'Malta.'

'Uhuh. With Stephen Garland. That much I gathered. Something about drowning.'

I was remembering. 'Retired major. Had a little villa above Valetta. Place swarming with kids. Grandchildren. His son was there for the summer. We'd gone out to question him—the major—about something nasty I'd dug up on Crete. It was awkward—those kids milling around all the time.' Dream and memory were flooding back now. Anne waited patiently. 'So Garland hired this fishing boat and the three of us went along the coast a mile or two. But, soon as the questions started, the man went beserk. Clobbered me with a mop handle and then turned on Garland. I picked myself up just in time to see him going over the side.'

'Garland?'

'No—the other fellow. Garland just stood there watching him. Sank like a stone—no struggle . . . nothing. I staggered across the deck, all set to go in and grab him, but Garland stopped me. The sea was clear as crystal just there. I could see the poor devil going down and down. Garland was gripping me like a gorilla. Then he let me go—and cursed me for behaving like a fool.'

Anne pushed back the damp hair from my forehead.

'So I should think ! You can't swim a stroke.'

Instinctive reaction. But Garland could swim like a fish. Said he wasn't going to risk being dragged down by a determined suicide. Seemed reasonable at the time. Since then . . .' I took a deep breath. The horror of the dream was sinking back into my unconscious like that distorted face on the end of its chain of bubbles . . . drifting down to the dark. 'So there it was. Tragic accident. Deepest regrets. Sad end to a fine military career.'

She set my head back on the pillow. 'But . . ?'

'His son didn't believe us. It showed.' I yawned. 'God—that was vivid. And it's all of twelve years ago.'

She leaned over and kissed me. 'Ancient history, professor.'

By morning the nightmare had lost its sting. Radio forecasts warned of thundery showers in distant parts of the country but for us the sun blazed relentlessly from a cloudless sky. At a steady four miles to the hour we moved west by south across the green heart of England. Much of the day Clare stood on the after deck, tiller tucked comfortably under her arm, responding to every whim of *Plantagent's* long hull. Overnight study of Nicholson's *Guide to the Waterways* had imbued the girl with some small enthusiasm for life on the Cut.

Late that afternoon we came to Tongstone.

Saint Gilbert of Sempringham died in 1188, holy and full of years—one hundred of them, to be precise. An innovator. our Gilbert—founding monasteries which housed both men and women. Canons and nuns each had their own cloisters and only met in the church which stood at the heart of the complex. If *met* is the right word for a congregation segregated by an eight foot wall down the middle of its place of worship. But such were the ways of the Gilbertines—the only wholly English monastic order of the Middle Ages.

Tongstone Priory, founded in 1180, flourished for three centuries then gradually declined. At the Visitation of 1536 the monastery was valued at seventy-five pounds, three shillings and fourpence—around a hundred and thirty dollars on the international market. Not bad for an acre of mediaeval masonry, complete with fixtures and fittings, all set in another five hundred acres of rolling country on which a thousand sheep were fattening.

Dissolution—at the behest of Defender of the Faith Henry VIII—was civilized business for Tongstone. Five canons and four nuns remained in cloisters built to house fifty. Offered handsome pensions, they accepted with alacrity and departed—some to complete their allotted span in conjugal bliss.

The site and its appurtenances were granted to the Oxshott family who demolished the monastic buildings and raised a mansion which passed to the Garlands a century later. Of the once-splendid edifice, all was now a roofless shell except the west wing where Stephen and Beth Garland lived in modest comfort—if twelve bedrooms and five reception rooms is your idea of modesty.

From *Plantagenet's* cabin top I gazed across parched meadows to the great house, its stonework grey-gold in the early evening sun. To the left of the Tudor mansion, crumbling walls marked the site of the Gilbertine monastery. As I watched, a large white tourist coach came into view, moving slowly towards the house.

Clare followed its progress through my binoculars. 'Your friend has visitors. *Hurrah for the Stately Homes of England!*'

Before dinner we took a stroll along the towpath. Clare was something of a naturalist and we spent an hour identifying flora and fauna of hedgerow and river bank. It was a relief to see the girl so engrossed. I made a mental note to buy a naturalist's handbook at the next bookstore we encountered. Aboard *Plantagenet* our library was limited to my historical reference books and Anne's collection of Dickens and Jane Austen—none of which held much appeal for our young guest.

It was on our return that we met Garland. He strode towards us along the towpath—a towering figure, angrily slashing a heavy walking-stick at nettles and cowparsley.

'Well met, *Charles Ridyard!*' He would have passed without a word had I not spoken. Ridyard was a departmental fiction cloaking our separate identities. His signature—a rubber stamp—appeared on our official correspondence.

Garland spun round, glaring short-sightedly—his whole body tense like an animal at bay.

'Who—?' Then suddenly he was smiling. '*David Meynell,* of all people. Well met indeed!' He gripped my hand warmly. 'And Mrs Meynell.' The shapeless tweed hat was snatched from his head for a sweeping bow. 'Your servant, ma'am. And . . . who's this young lady? Surely no progeny of thine, young David?'

'A guest, I said guardedly. 'Department business—believe it or not.'

He chuckled. 'Oh, I believe it. I'd believe anything of the old firm.' He raised his hat to Clare. 'Anonymous guest, I salute you.'

She smiled. 'I'm pleased to make your acquaintance, Mr Garland.'

He stepped back in mock astonishment. 'An American—and she knows my name. Such are the fruits of notoriety! Anonymous American guest, thrice welcome to my humble acres.' He moved closer and whispered confidentially, 'What's a nice girl like you doing in a place like this in Bicentennial Year? You should be back home celebrating your deliverance from wicked old Tories like me. Come to think of it—what brings *you* to Tongstone, David?'

I pointed to where *Plantagenet* lay alongside the tow-path. He shaded his eyes against the sun. 'Ha! *You're* the blighter who leaves mooring lines strung across the public footpath. Nearly broke my neck. But—you're not the nautical type.'

'The Old Man's idea. Remember that book I told you about—the guide to defence properties? He wants it by October. *Plantagenet* belongs to one of his friends. A month afloat. Peace and quiet. Get the book finished. Sounds great, doesn't it? *You* try creative writing when you're steering, working through locks and generally keeping things shipshape. See how far you get. I'm no further than Chapter Three.'

He nodded towards the canal. 'Drought restrictions must be the answer to a writer's prayer. You'll be the only skipper who isn't cursing the Waterways Board regulations.'

'A mixed blessing. We've spent the night in some odd places—alongside gasworks or at the back of a disco.'

He stroked his beard. 'Ah, well, that's all over now. I congratulate you on your final mooring. With the Priory as backdrop to your literary endeavour, you'll write as one inspired. I speak from experience. And if you want a change of scene, my study is at your disposal.'

Any other time I would have accepted his tempting invitation without hesitation. But until the threat to Clare was past, we must keep moving.

'We hadn't planned to stay long.'

'But *force majeure* cannot be denied, what?'

I stared at him.

'The restrictions, man, the restrictions. Don't tell me you haven't heard? As from seven o'clock tonight the canal is closed till further notice. No craft allowed through any lock.' He pointed towards *Plantagenet*. 'You're stuck right *there* till the rains come.'

CHAPTER THREE

We invited him aboard for a drink. While Anne tidied the saloon and I set bottles and glasses on the table, Clare took him on a tour of inspection. Their laughter and animated conversation reached us through the thin bulk-heads.

Anne pitched a sweater through the open door into our stateroom. 'That's the first time I've heard her laugh since she arrived. Do the Garlands have any family?'

'No. Big disappointment to Stephen, but I'm not so sure about Beth. She's a good bit younger than he is—and something of a career woman.'

'Chauvinist!'

Over drinks, Garland amplified his invitation. 'I'll have to be an absentee host for the next few days. First thing tomorrow I'm off to join Beth in Scotland. They've had a fair drop of rain up there, so I should manage some fishing. We go every year. But feel free to use the Priory while I'm away. We'll be back by the middle of next week. Can't be away too long, with the harvest so early this year—and it's a busy time for Beth. Got herself a job with the Tourist Board, y'know.' He smiled ruefully. 'If she had her way the Priory would be—what does she call it?— *a cultural centre for the discerning overseas visitor.* In other words, a swanky tourist hotel. Well, I've compromised. We open the doors to *hoi polloi* on Wednesdays and Saturdays. Believe me, that's enough. Just got rid of a crowd of 'em. That's why I stepped outside for a breath of fresh air. The stupid questions they ask! But that won't concern you. While I'm away, Mrs Frost does the honours for our esteemed clientele. A formidable woman! Comes in from the village every day. Took her on as a daily help for Beth. Now she's made herself indispensable. *La grande chatelaine.*' He glanced at his watch. 'I'd ask you over for dinner, only the prospect of catering for three guests at short notice would not find favour in Mrs Frost's eyes.'

'Stay for a meal with us,' suggested Anne.

His hands flew up in horror. 'My dear girl!' he protested. 'You know not what you ask. Were I a free man, nothing would keep me from your gracious board. As things are—Mrs Frost would regard my rejection of her shepherd's pie as the most unkind cut of all. That woman *terrorises* me! Beth knows how to handle her, but me she exploits mercilessly. In any case, I have to get back. Expecting my—a visitor. But come across after dinner. I'll show you round and let you have a set of keys.' He stood up—his bulky form dominating the saloon. 'Come right in. No use ringing the doorbell, it's packed up. Damned electrician was supposed to fix it today. Not a sign of him. Typical! See you . . . around eight-thirty?'

We saw him ashore and stood watching him stride away towards the Priory. At the gate leading to the meadows he turned and waved.

Clare sighed. 'Can we really stay at the Priory? He says it's haunted.' Her eyes grew dreamy. *'A dark wraith rising from the desecrated chapel and drifting across moonlit lawns, its accusing finger outstretched towards the silent house.'*

The expensive sound of powerful marine engines interrupted her dramatic soliloquy and drew our eyes along the canal. Gleaming white hull . . . varnished superstructure . . . searchlight . . . dinghy in davits at the stern—the craft radiated disdain for the narrow confines of that inland waterway. The engines opened up in a quick surge of power while water boiled white at the stern. Pulled up short by the reverse thrust of twin propellers, the cruiser bobbed a curtsey and edged slowly towards the bank, twenty yards from where we were moored. I could see the helmsman at his impressive controls in the wheelhouse but no crew appeared on deck, ready to jump ashore with ropes. Beneath a drooping Red Ensign, the vessel's name was blazoned proudly across her stern. *CZARINA—LONDON*.

I hurried along the towpath. The man had misjudged his approach and *Czarina's* wash was pushing her away from the bank. Another quick burst from the engines and she was bearing down on me. Again reverse dragged her back until she lay athwart the canal, rocking violently on the disturbed waters.

I gave an encouraging wave. 'Throw me a line.'

Crowned by an immaculate yachting cap, the skipper's flushed face appeared at the wheelhouse door. 'Do what?'

I pointed to his foredeck where a mooring line lay loosely coiled. 'Throw me a rope. I'll tow you in.'

'Oh—thanks.' He scrambled clumsily on to the narrow side-deck and hurried forward. A moment later the rope sailed through the air and dropped noisily into the water three feet from the bank. Success came with his third attempt. Hand over hand, I drew the dripping line ashore.

'Fine craft.' I thrust away the bows to bring the boat broadside against the bank.

'Not so dusty,' he mumbled. His yachting cap had slipped to a rakish angle over one eye. Peter Pan with a weight problem. Twenty-five, with a paunch his natty blazer did nothing to conceal. Fleshy cheeks and double chin added years to his appearance, while heaving chest and whistling breath revealed a man sadly out of condition. But his grin was entirely boyish. Appreciation of his boat was accepted as personal compliment. Clutching the stumpy pennant-mast he leaned against the fore-cabin like a transatlantic yachtsman posing after a successful lone crossing. 'Wasted in this glorified ditch,' he gasped scornfully. 'You should see her get up and go, offshore.' Clawing his way aft he tossed me the stern rope. 'Come aboard?'

Czarina was like a floating emporium of ship's chandlery. Her instrumentation resembled the flight-deck of a jumbo jet. With a proud wave of his podgy hand he indicated the overpowering array of dials and levers. Depth-sounder . . . doppler speed log . . . direction-finder . . . radio telephone—all ranged before the massive wheel. On the chart table, an electronic calculator programmed for trigonometry.

I tapped the chart. 'Optimist. You won't be seeing the North Sea this summer.'

He cackled wheezily. 'Never heard of mobile cranes and transporter trucks?'

Below deck *Czarina* was fitted with every refinement for long-distance cruising. Mirrors and gleaming varnish created an illusion of space in a craft thirty feet shorter than *Plantagenet* and no broader in the beam. She could accommodate four in comfort, two in luxury.

Back in the wheelhouse, I said, 'Looks as though we'll be neighbours for a while. I'm David Meynell.'

'Colin Wright.' He glared bitterly at the tranquil canal. 'Blasted restrictions. So much for our statutory right of navigation. We're only here on sufferance—and don't they just love to let us know it?'

Over dinner aboard *Plantagenet* discussion centred on our new neighbour and his trim command.

'I've met his type, back home,' said Clare loftily—the maturity of her tone countered by the youthful appetite with which she was attacking her strawberries and cream. 'Thinks handling a powerboat is like driving a car. If you hadn't been around, he'd still be trying to get ashore.'

I nodded. 'Radar . . . North Sea charts—who's he kidding? He's been no further out to sea than the end of Blackpool pier.'

There was no sign of life aboard *Czarina* when we set out for the Priory.

'Gone for a meal at the nearest pub,' I suggested. 'Doubt if he could even boil himself an egg.'

For a tranquil summer evening the countryside was remarkably noisy. From neighbouring fields came the roar of tractors and combine-harvesters—dwindling as the lumbering machines moved slowly out of sight behind clumps of trees or sank over the horizon of nearby hillocks, then rising in crescendo as they reappeared. From time to time the sharp report of a shotgun or a sporting rifle drifted across the meadows. With rabbits multiplying again after myxomatosis, harvest sport had returned. Before the clattering combines, dozens of tiny creatures had retreated within the ever-dwindling area of standing corn until panic drove them blindly from cover—to be shot down as they bounded across the stubble. I had not witnessed such a scene since my childhood just after the war.

Approaching the Priory we could see the full extent of the fire which gutted the main rooms on a summer's night forty years earlier. Looking up through blind mullioned windows which flanked an imposing doorway we glimpsed ornate Tudor fireplaces, weathered and crumbling. Higher still, mean hearths at which chilled domestics had huddled from searching draughts.

The house itself—magnificent in its day—was a ghostly shadow of glory now departed. Clare was enraptured and eager to ignore the ominous *KEEP OUT —DANGER OF FALLING MASONRY* board beside the gaping doorway.

The broad drive must once have been covered with oft-raked gravel, but this had been replaced by drab asphalt blotched with rainbow-hued oilstains.

The long-dead architect's symmetry had been sacrificed by the creation of a new entrance in the facade of the west wing. Today's planning pundits would reject this concession to convenience, but Stephen Garland's father held to the outmoded creed that an Englishman's home is a castle with which he may do as he pleases.

The occupied wing, at right angles to the central bulk of the building, had been in shadow since early afternoon, yet its mellow stonework still radiated warmth.

Through the open door we stepped into a cool stone-flagged hall, some thirty feet square—its proportions enhanced by a low decorated plaster ceiling. From panelled walls ancestral portraits regarded us with the polite disdain their station in life demanded. In overlarge frames they dominated the hall and had clearly been commissioned to grace loftier surroundings. I guessed they had been salvaged from the grand stair at the time of the fire.

To our left an open door revealed book-lined walls, easy chairs and a rich marble fireplace. Garland's study. Our host was waiting for us, seated at his ease beside the empty grate, his back to the door and his wing chair partly hidden by an elegant eighteenth-century green leather screen. I could just see his left hand resting along the tapestry-covered arm. From a record-player on the low table beside him a coiled wire stretched to his stereo headphones. Insulated from all extraneous sounds he was unaware of our presence. In that brief moment I envied him—not his grand house or broad acres . . . not even that bookish den and the old easy chair with stuffing bursting from a hole in its back. I envied him the tranquil knowledge that he was beyond reach of the Director and all his works.

I stepped forward to greet him—and all envy fled.

Beyond reach of the Director, Stephen Garland was past all human contact. Where his right eye had been there was now a gaping hole from which blood ran down the wreckage of his face and onto his tweed jacket.

CHAPTER FOUR

Like models for a sculptured group depicting *Horror* we stood . . . frozen . . . aghast. Not a word was uttered. We stared at the corpse. We stared at each other. All colour drained from Clare's face until it had the appearance of sculptor's marble. Then—breaking in on the oppressive silence—we caught the sound of footsteps pattering down the stairs.

Impulse drove us behind the green leather screen, its rococo top embellished with glass panels set in elegant curved wooden frames. Through these I could see the door which opened towards us, blocking our view into the hall. As I watched, a revolver appeared round the edge of that door.

With a sense of detachment—as though viewing action on television—I recognised the ventilated barrel of a Colt Python six-shot. A connoisseur's choice among handguns, it was grasped by a man wearing a dark blue blazer. I saw his hand . . . the cuff of his shirt . . . and a gilded button on his sleeve. Then—and only then—did I realize the simplest of physical facts. If that glass allowed me to see the armed man, it afforded him equal opportunity to see me.

Say I was still confused by what had happened. Say I was hypnotized by that slowly-thrusting Python. Better still, say I was a fool.

I ducked—my eyes now level with Garland's shattered face. Only a firearm could disfigure like that. No wonder the padding had burst from the back of his chair. Half his brain must have lodged in the upholstery. I had met the sight before—in reality and in illustrated manuals of forensic medicine.

In the stillness I could hear wheezy breathing from the man by the door. Two paces—and discovery was certain. Five shots in that Colt? Three of us behind the screen. In such circumstances five into three *will* go—with deadly effect.

Doctor Johnson was right. *Depend upon it, Sir, when a man knows he is to be hanged in a fortnight, it concentrates his mind wonderfully.* Hanged in a fortnight or shot in three seconds—the effect is the same. I have total recall of those moments behind the screen. I see thickening blood still drip from Garland's beard and hear again the thin whisper of music from his headphones. His skull was now an emptied cavity yet into his deadened ears poured solemn melody—Variation Nine from Elgar's *Enigma*, the musical portrait of the composer's friend A. E. Jaeger—*Nimrod*. I can even remember the bright picture that flashed into my mind as I recognized that music. I was a boy again, striding beside my father across Elgar's beloved Malvern hills.

All that in three seconds. Then the footsteps moved away across the hall.

Breathless, we waited the longest minute I remember—then crept from our hiding place. Distant sounds told us our unwelcome visitor was searching across the hall. I pointed towards the front door. One headlong dash for the garden . . .

But even as we braced ourselves, the stillness of that room of death was shattered by strident clangour. The phone.

I pictured the armed man hurrying towards the study. Reason would have known he too was thrown off-balance by that unexpected din. But reason was elsewhere just then. Desperation dragged us to a mullioned window where one large leaded section stood wide, letting in cool breezes and the distant sounds of harvest.

With that phone ringing a tocsin of doom, we scrambled through the open window, dropped lightly on to a flower bed and raced to the old monastic buildings where we crouched in what had once been the sacristy—a stone cubicle off the sanctuary of the ruined chapel.

Anne touched my arm. 'Who was it?' she whispered.

'I only saw the gun he was holding.'

Clare shivered. 'It was the man on the boat.'

I stared at her. 'Wright? You're sure?'

She nodded miserably, 'I could see through the crack in that screen.'

Colour was coming back to her cheeks. Our mad rush across the garden had purged shock from her system. So—she was a prime witness, but to what purpose? Her safety outweighed any obligation to the dead Garland. To reveal her presence to the police would be to make it common knowledge—something my orders would not permit.

Above us a narrow window looked east towards the house. Centuries before, the smooth facing of the sacristy walls had been filched to build the mansion. To climb the remaining rough blocks was easy. A grip here . . . a toehold there.

Ten feet up . . . and my hands were grasping the base of the window's mediaeval tracery. Slowly . . . *very* slowly . . . I raised my head—to look directly at the western face of the house. Hundreds of leaded diamond panes threw back dazzling rays from the setting sun. I blinked—and at that moment the sound of a shot leaped at me from the house and smacked loudly against the lofty wall of the chapel.

My descent was precipitate and painful. For a few seconds I stared stupidly at my torn and bleeding hands, then we were away down the shadowed chapel, rushing along the avenue of once-vaulting pillars. Beyond, the meadow sloped to a stream, hidden from any eyes at the Priory.

What the military manuals call *dead ground.*

Dread faded with each step as we walked across fields where men were harvesting and guns were fired in sport and not in anger. And with growing security our sense of proportion returned. I put myself in Colin Wright's position. He must assume we had recognized him. Within minutes the police would be alerted and he become a hunted man. To pursue us now would be an act of folly. We would be safe aboard *Plantagenet.* Twenty minutes after leaving the Priory I was sitting on the saloon sofa while Anne gave my injured hands the Band-aid treatment.

I waggled swathed fingers clumsily. 'I'm going to have fun working the phone dial with these.'

She was repacking the first-aid kit. 'Use a pencil. Calling the office?'

'They'll want to know about Garland. He may have resigned, but there's still a file on him. And we've a material witness on our hands. Hey—where *is* Clare?'

A call from the deck answered my question. 'Come and take a look.'

She was on the cabin top, studying the Priory through

my binoculars. I scrambled up beside her and took them awkwardly in my bandaged hands. 'What am I supposed to be looking at ?'

'A jeep. Came from the house. Boy—was it moving!'

The roving lenses picked up a cloud of dust rising to the left of the building and a blurred shape speeding along the far side of a hedge. It flashed across an open gateway.

'Landrover. Going round the edge of that field. You're right—he *is* shifting. Sailor-boy must be in a sweat—and I'll bet he's got poor old Garland's body with him.' I turned to the girl. 'I'm sorry about all this, Clare.'

'I'll be okay. Everything happened so *fast*. I don't think it's really hit me yet. What are we to do? We can't stay here as though nothing's happened.'

Twenty minutes later I was talking to Ron Metcalfe from the village callbox. Down the line came muffled crunching like brittle thunder. Ron was thrashing the Rennies—and short on sympathy for our plight.

'There's a curse on the house of Meynell!' Exasperation set an edge to his voice. 'I'm not kidding, boyo. You're letting this kind of thing become a habit. Every time, it's the same—you take a perfectly straightforward operation and proceed to screw it horrid. Your job was to drift peacefully down the canals, minding your own business and keeping out of sight until we gave the word. Nothing said about hob-nobbing with the landed gentry—especially someone like Stephen Garland.'

'I simply wanted his advice as a writer. Damn it, he *was* one of us.'

'He was—and now he wants the whole world to know.

His autobiography is a very indiscreet document. Too much detail about the old firm. We're trying to hold up publication. Garland kicked at that, so we've had to send somebody up there to try a spot of friendly persuasion on the old fool.'

'Oh God!' I said softly. 'Not a fat kid who calls himself Colin Wright?'

'You should know better than to ask.' The bantering tone had gone. 'Where are you calling from?'

'Phone box in Tongstone.' I read the number on the dial. 'Furzeby 317.'

'Furzeby? Ouch! I don't like the sound of that, old son. Indeed I do not. Big American air base around there. With Clare Patterson in tow, that's a place to avoid. You say you can't shift that floating bath-tub of yours? Right—here's what you do. Get back to Anne and the kid. Stay put tonight but be ready to move out. I'll call the Old Man. That may take time. He's somewhere in the wilds of Nova Scotia with the Royals right now, but we'll work something out. Call me here, first thing in the morning—and I mean first thing. Make it five o'clock. Check?'

'Check. I'll call at five. See you.'

'Not if I see you first, mate.'

The village pub was disgorging customers as I left the callbox. *Goodnights* to Harry, Sue, George and half the drinking population of Tongstone echoed along the ill-lit street. In surrounding fields, combines and tractors were still at work, headlights blazing. Mist was rising from the canal and down on the towpath the air was chill. I walked briskly, anxious to get back and reassure the others. As I rounded a bend, the lights of *Plantagenet* welcomed me while quadraphonic hi-fi brought John Denver beside still waters. Further along the bank lay *Czarina*, darkened and silent.

As I reached our gangplank a figure stepped from the shadow of the hedge and flashed a light into my face.

'Excuse me, sir. This your boat?'

The police had arrived.

CHAPTER FIVE

I showed him my Ministry pass and explained about *Plantagenet*. He was in his forties and heavily built—a constable well content with the policeman's lot. Patrol car work, to judge from his peaked cap.

'Been here long, sir?'

'Arrived just after tea. About five o'clock. Not moored in the wrong place, am I?'

'No sir. Quite in order to tie up on towpath side. We're just checking on people in neighbourhood. There's been some trouble—over way.' He nodded towards the Priory.

'Garland's place?'

'Know gentleman, sir?' In his clipped speech all definite articles were swallowed, emerging as hesitant gulps before the nouns.

'We worked together for some years. Kept in touch ever since. *Trouble?* What—somebody run off with his silver?'

He cleared his throat. 'Sight more serious than that. Mr Garland's dead.'

Don't over-react. 'Dead? Since when? He was here this evening.'

'What time would that be, about?'

I rubbed my forehead with a bandaged hand. 'Six? Could have been nearer quarter past, perhaps. Can't be more precise.'

'And you last saw him—when?' A ballpoint hovered over his notebook.

'We asked him aboard for a drink. He wouldn't stay for dinner, but we nattered for a while. Could have been about seven when he left.'

'Left . . . about . . . seven.' He spoke slowly as he wrote the words. 'How did he seem, when he left you?'

'Quite cheerful. He'd invited us over to the Priory tomorrow morning. Matter of fact, he'd invited us to use his place while he was away in Scotland. These latest water restrictions have put the lid on our cruising.'

His eyes narrowed and he looked at me sharply. 'Definitely invited you to Priory, did he?'

'Yes. Look here—what's happened? Has there been an accident or something?'

He did not look up from his notebook. 'I'm not at liberty to say, sir. Mind if I ask where you've just been?'

'Down to the village. Had to make a phone call.'

'You're not alone on this boat, seemingly.'

'My wife's with me.'

He jerked a thumb towards *Czarina*. 'Anything to do with you?'

'No—she belongs to a chap called Colin Wright. Turned up this evening, just after Garland left.'

'Mr Wright? Ah—we know *that* gentleman.'

By midnight we were packed. Clare was exhausted—overtired. Reaction had set in, making her fractious and petulant. Everything was wrong—her quarters cramped and inconvenient . . . her lack of fresh clothes humiliating. She found our domestic foibles irritating . . . our meals taken at uncivilized hours . . . our food unfamiliar. In a brittle voice she vented unreasoned scorn on the innocent custom of afternoon tea. At that hour of the night my riposte about the legendary Boston party was ill-timed. We understood . . . we sympathised—but it was with relief that we heard her cabin door slam shut. I took a last turn round the deck, checked our mooring lines and dragged the gangplank inboard. Then I joined Anne in our stateroom, set the alarm for four-thirty, climbed wearily into bed and switched out the light.

My father's long strides were leaving me far behind. About us stretched the Malverns, yet here was Leptis Magna—North African Rome among English hills. And the ancient city lived again. Chariots . . . togas . . . a centurion in plumaged helmet. CAVE CANEM—there ran the dog whose pawmarks on wet clay tiles would be cherished in a dozen museums. Ahead, my father, clad now as a gladiator, turned and stared at me with Garland's shattered face—the blood still wet on cheek and jaw—while from a shadowed arch Anne whispered urgently, 'David! David!'

'*David!*' Her lips were close to my ear. 'Somebody's out there on the towpath.'

I stared blankly at the curtained window, pale in predawn twilight. *Towpath?* I was still in Leptis Magna. Twisting my head I saw the luminous dial of the alarm. Three fifteen.

Furtive scrabbling near our stern . . . a gentle rocking of *Plantagenet's* long hull—someone was trying to board. Beyond a gap in the curtains the towpath hedge slid sideways then retreated as we moved away from the bank. Snatching a bathrobe from behind the cabin door I padded along the narrow passage to the aft companionway. Beyond the bolted door, our nocturnal visitor had abandoned hope of silent arrival. Grunts . . . more scrabbling and a violent lurch were followed by a loud metallic thud which echoed through the boat. Then came the splash of a heavy body landing in the canal.

Silence.

Then a voice, slowly and systematically invoking curses which grew ever more comprehensive—widening ripples from a stone cast in a still lake. Whispered venom cursed my name and ancestry . . . *Plantagenet* . . . every floating craft known to man . . . the whole waterways system, rivers, sea—and all that therein is . . .

I unbolted the door and stuck my head out. *'Who dat down dere?'*

Chest-deep in water, Ron Metcalfe glared up at me.

I dragged him aboard—pungent with primordial ooze . . . helped him strip off his sodden clothes . . . then led him below for a hot shower. He squelched into the tiny bathroom and banged the door.

'Go easy with the water,' I warned. 'We're running low on reserves.'

The door slid back violently. *'What?'*

'We're short of water.'

He opened his mouth but said nothing—eloquently. Then he picked a frond of weed from his damp chin and retired behind the door to thrash our meagre liquid reserves.

Even after coffee laced with rum he was tetchy.

'Look at that!' he fumed, slapping a sodden Rennies packet on the saloon table. 'My life-support system ruined. Go ahead and laugh while you can, you ditch-crawler. All packed up and ready for off are you? Marvellous. Now put everything back the way it was.

You're not going anywhere.' He leaned back and sipped his coffee with malevolent relish.

I looked at him suspiciously. 'You're taking Clare off our hands?'

For answer he rummaged the damp contents of his pockets, now spread on the table, and selected a stained envelope. 'All in there, boyo.'

I peeled open the flap and tugged out a blotched sheet of Ministry notepaper. It was a transcript of the Director's orders as they had bounced off the mid-Atlantic satellite into Ron's phone.

I require and expect immediate action to establish the identity of the person or persons responsible for Stephen Garland's death. This is now Meynell's prime concern but at no time shall he act in such a way as to compromise the security of the operation upon which he is already engaged. Speed is of the essence of this investigation since those favourable conditions which currently pertain may reasonably be expected to deteriorate rapidly.

Having regard to the circumstances reported to me, the duty armourer is to issue the following: Item—one five-shot Smith and Wesson 38 special. Item—one small box low-penetration ammunition for same. Item—one shoulder holster . . .

Glancing up from the limp paper I caught Ron's grin.

'And you?' I asked.

'Back-up. And in the very limited time at my disposal I've been doing my homework. Wright's not one of ours. The Old Man's anxious to know if Garland's death links in with any of the jobs he pulled in the old days. That business in Malta, for instance. You were there. All very unsatisfactory. I've been on to computers for a printout of every TCO assignment Garland handled. File abstracts should be here by courier any time. Somewhere among that lot we may find your friend Wright.'

I shook my head. 'Garland resigned ten years ago. Wright would have been about fifteen, then.'

'Impressionable age. If we're dealing with a vendetta—what? Are you suggesting Wright's a professional?'

Anne pushed back her hair with a gesture of irritation. 'Why does everything *have* to revolve round the Department? This business will probably turn out to be a squalid local scandal.'

Ron stood up stiffly and opened the briefcase I had fetched aboard from the towpath. 'Let's hope you're right. Anyway—that's what your husband's going to find out for us, aren't you, old sport? And don't forget—*speed is of the essence.* Me—I'm for a kip. Wake me around mid-day. You should have lots to tell me by then. But first—your signature for these.' He dipped in the case and brought out the Smith and Wesson, the ammunition and a sweat-stained holster. 'This is what they mean by cuts in public spending,' he muttered. 'Last year we'd have had a popgun apiece.'

I signed a receipt and showed Ron to his cramped cabin next to Clare's. When I returned to the saloon Anne was still seated at the table, staring at the revolver. She ran her finger lightly along its stubby two-inch barrel.

'*My* husband is an archaeologist,' she murmured. 'My husband *is* an archaeologist. My husband is an *archaeologist.* D'you think, if I say that often enough, I'll convince myself? Things don't get any better, do they, David? When you took over D19 they promised it would be a safe job—one you're actually qualified for. But *this*—'

I held the gun in my bandaged hand. 'Know what the Old Man told me, once? I'm a man things *happen* to. Ron's convinced I possess magnetic attraction for trouble.'

'Darling, it doesn't just come—it's *sent.* And who sends it?'

I reached to smooth the anxious line between her golden eyebrows. 'Being around when Garland was killed—that's just bad luck.'

She tossed her head. 'We'd be fifty miles further on if you hadn't been called to Boston. And whose idea was that? He's pushing you right back into the firing line. And this is how it'll be—every time.'

'So why don't I get out and take that job your father wrote us about, huh?'

Her shoulders drooped. 'I didn't *say* that, David. There's nothing wrong with D19, and this writing you're doing opens up all sorts of possibilities. But you're not allowed to do your job. What kind of state will you be in when this wretched business is over? Darling, I know what I'm talking about. I have to live with you. You go *grey*—know what I mean?—like a shadow. Half the time you're not really there at all. Then the nightmares start.'

I sat there, staring at the revolver—remembering those other times and their relentless aftermath. One persistent nightmare in particular. I would be watching a western on television. The film would be nearing its climax—that obligatory shoot-out on Main Street where *A Man's Gotta Do What A Man's Gotta Do.* And suddenly I would be part of the action, standing there on the street, gun in hand while my opponent faced me, fifty paces away. The bright sun threw bars of shadow across the highway and a wind from the desert filled the air with billowed dust, shrouding the figure of my foe. But his face was always clear . . . eyes staring . . . vengeful. And that face changed with each recurrence of the dream—always the victim of my latest assignment for the Department.

Childish? A psychiatrist might see it as acknowledgement of personal responsibilities for the results of my work. But no interpretation could exorcise the terror of those moments as I waited to exchange shots in cold blood. Mercifully I would waken before the lead started to fly. Always. Yet there was the constant dread that *this* time escape would be denied me as that distant figure took deliberate aim . . .

Anne's hand closed on mine. 'Darling, I'm sorry. Right now I ought to be boosting your confidence. Let's skip job-analysis and get you to work. What first? I'll fix that hand so you can use this artillery.'

Five-thirty. We dressed and waded through rising mist to examine *Czarina*. A floating enigma, ready for extended cruising in deep waters. Sophisticated navigation equipment . . . charts covering thousands of square nautical miles around the British coast . . . tanks full . . . radio tuned to a marine channel—yet the only sign of occupation, one cigar butt crushed into an ashtray in the wheel-house. No clothes in the capacious lockers or well-designed drawer-space. A gleaming galley, completely bare of provisions.

I closed the empty fridge. 'This doesn't make any kind of sense. If we were on the coast, this set-up would be ideal. High-powered cruiser all tanked up and ready for a quick getaway. But not here. It's not even as if he used the boat to sneak up on the Priory without being seen.

The way he arrived, you'd think he wanted the whole neighbourhood to know.'

As we strolled back to *Plantagenet* the smell of frying bacon came bowling along the towpath to greet us. Clare's surprised face looked out of the galley as we passed.

'Hi—early birds!' Sleep had eased away her late-night petulance. 'When do we leave?'

Amazingly she had slept through the alarms and excursions of the early morning. Over breakfast we brought her up to date with developments. If she was apprehensive, it did not show.

'What do we do next?' She was fighting a losing battle with an over-crisp rasher of bacon.

'*We?*' Anne raised an eyebrow. 'You, young woman, stay well out of sight.'

'Oh come *on*—you're not going to make me spend the whole day cooped up in here?'

'It's not up to us,' I said sympathetically. 'It's what your father wants. But you can make yourself useful. Fix some chow for Mr Metcalfe when he wakes up.'

'Big deal!'

'Okay—then how about this? That jeep we saw yesterday. Where did it go?'

I handed her our one-inch Ordance Survey map—an old copy salvaged from the Department's waste-bin. She spread it on the saloon floor and knelt to study it—but her efforts only deepened the mystery.

The one exit on the far side of that field was a level-crossing over the railway linking Brentwell Junction in the west with Furzeby and other stations further east, off the map. Beyond that crossing lay another field and another and another. Then the way was blocked by a stream meandering southwards to join the canalized River Wilde a short distance above our mooring.

Clare's finger tapped the *Ungated Crossing* symbol. 'Could he board a train there? I saw an old movie once about an English railroad. The engineer would stop anywhere, if you asked him.'

I was reluctant to destroy so delightful a myth. 'If those days ever existed, they're long gone.'

She looked up from the map, her face puzzled. 'Then where was he heading?'

CHAPTER
SIX

Nine o'clock. I was standing on the site of that crossing. East and west—as on the map—embankment and cutting stretched away to curve out of sight after a quarter of a mile in each direction.

But that map lied. The last train had long since rumbled round the bend and into oblivion. Encroaching vegetation told that the permanent way had been abandoned years before—rails lifted, sleepers removed, ballast carted away. What I now saw resembled a drover's road of bygone days—one of those ancient greenways down which cattle were driven to distant markets. Long unused, they may yet be traced—shrunken, overgrown relics of a network that once crossed and recrossed the kingdom.

Gazing along that forsaken railway I recalled the substance of lectures I had delivered. England abounds in hidden ways, from sunken lanes of prehistoric man to stretches of crumbling tarmac made redundant by the latest motorway. How often had I enthused on the magic of canals—water-filled veins and arteries forming a near-forgotten system across the length and breadth of the land. *Plantagenet* could sail through the heart of town and city almost unheeded—and of those who marked her passage, how many would realize that she swam upon a liquid highway which could carry her to London . . . Birmingham . . . Liverpool . . . York—almost any major city you care to name.

History moves on. As railways ousted canals so they in turn felt the withering blast of progress. The years brought closure to hundreds of miles of once-busy track—and with that closure, slow oblivion. Out of use . . . out of sight . . . out of mind. Men turned their backs on the abandoned lines.

But someone had taken account of this forgotten track. Deep ruts showed where heavy vehicles passed in wet weather. Lighter imprints in the dust told of traffic in recent dry days.

Chesterton was right. The rolling English drunkard made the rolling English road. It staggers and meanders along the line of ancient hard-contended boundaries. But men who build railways hold to the geometric principle that the shortest distance between two points is a straight line. From Tongstone Priory to Brentwell by road would take a car twenty minutes. Along the abandoned railway a jeep could reach that same destination in half the time.

Turning towards the Priory I crunched across stubble where rectangular straw bales lay scattered like ammunition boxes on an abandoned battlefield.

My arrival at the house coincided with that of a dark blue police van. I recognised the driver—my questioner of the night before. I saw him speak to the man beside him and a moment later his companion was out of the van and striding towards me.

'Mr Meynell? I'm Pollard. Had a message just now to say you're investigating on behalf of MOD—right?'

I nodded. The man—in sergeant's uniform—looked no older than his driver but there was a marked contrast between the two. One would be content to draw a constable's pension—the other had his sights on higher things. It would not be easy to hide anything from his beady professional eyes.

'Don't let me get in your way,' I said diplomatically.

'I've been asked to prepare a report on Stephen Garland's death. He'd worked for us and we keep tabs on all our personnel. Can you put me in the picture?'

He led the way towards the house. 'How much did Redgrave tell you?'

'Your driver? Not a lot.'

'Yes—well, he had his instructions. We found the body last night.'

'Where?'

He looked surprised. 'Why, here of course. Where else? Just after ten. I'd told Mr Garland we'd look in some time during the evening. We keep an eye on the place whenever he's away and we usually pay him a call before he goes, just to check what arrangements he's made about the keys and so on. He's got a lot of valuable stuff lying around here, you know. Big temptation—not just for your professional villain but for local layabouts. So—we arrived around ten. Tried the bell—no reply.'

'It's out of order.'

He looked at me sharply. 'How come you know that?'

'Garland told me. He'd invited us over this morning. Told us to walk straight in because the bell wasn't working.'

'I see. Well, that's what we did. Walked straight in—and there he was, in the study. Dead about an hour, according to our pathologist.'

'But . . . *how?*'

'Shot. Thought you knew. He'd blown his brains out.'

* * *

Inside the house strident pop music jarred the ear.

'Turn that row off!' The sergeant's voice echoed through the building. Sudden silence was followed by the appearance of a shamefaced young constable at the study door.

My companion glared. 'Use a bit of common, son. Mrs Garland's due back any time. She won't want that racket.'

I followed him into Garland's den. The place struck chill—unwarmed by the morning sun which was just topping the roofless ruin of the east wing.

'This where it happened?' I gazed round as though seeing the room for the first time.

'Right here.' His hand rested lightly on the back of the wing chair.

'And you're sure it was suicide?'

He pinched the tip of his nose and frowned slightly. 'I knew you'd say something like that.'

'He had enemies.'

'Who hasn't? But that's theorizing. We go by the evidence—and that points fair and square to a simple choice between accident and suicide. When we found him last night he was sitting in this chair, wearing those head-phones, with a revolver in his lap and his face shot to blazes.'

'A revolver?' I recalled the weapon in Wright's hand.

'His own—and duly licensed. He's got a regular arsenal along there in the gunroom. This was a hefty job—bit like the old service issue. What they call a Colt magnum. Ring a bell with you?'

'He didn't get it from us, if that's what you're asking.'

He gave a knowing smile. 'Thought not. Shade too obvious for your kind of work, eh?'

'It was in his lap?'

He nodded. 'Mr Garland knew how to handle fire-arms but accidents do happen. He used both hands—holding the thing back to front, if you follow me. Both hands round the butt . . . right thumb on the trigger. Last thing he saw was the view down the barrel.'

'But was it deliberate?'

He touched my arm and led me out of earshot of the young constable. 'Here's how it looks. Mrs Garland away . . . the house empty—right? Ideal for anyone who wants to do away with himself without distressing a lot of people. But *somebody's* going to find the body—like it might be Mrs Frost coming in, this morning. She does for the Garlands, if you follow. Now Garland knew we'd be calling, last evening. Is that the way he wanted it—rather than have Mrs Frost screaming her head off all the way to Tongstone?'

'Can't you be sure?'

'No—and if I start hinting at suicide without adequate evidence, I'm in trouble. You see—' He hesitated. 'There's something missing.'

'Robbery?'

'No—nothing like that. I'm talking about a suicide note. There isn't one. As things stand, we've nothing to *prove* Garland took his own life. The coroner's not going to concern himself with my gut reaction. Without conclusive proof, he'll record a misadventure verdict.'

'You've searched?'

'Thoroughly. Matter of routine. Went over the place from cellar to attic. Not just for a suicide note, of course. For anything—*odd*. Got to keep an open mind.'

'And—?'

'*Nothing*. Have to check with Mrs Garland, of course

—when she gets back. Now . . . that's a point. You know her well? Well enough to break the news, I mean?'

'Break—? Hasn't she been told?'

'Only that there's been an accident and her husband's dead. The local police up at Glencairn got her on the night train.' He glanced at his watch. 'She could be here within the hour.'

'Afraid I can't stop more than a few minutes.' Concealing my knowledge from this sergeant was one thing. Lying to Stephen Garland's widow was something else.

So now I knew why Colin Wright had delayed his departure from the Priory. He had used the time to create an illusion so cleverly staged that even the police were deceived. Yet even as I thought about it, fresh doubts rose in my mind. I could not believe Wright just *happened* to call at the Priory when his victim was so completely at his mercy. A platoon of booted assassins could have stamped into the study unheard as long as Garland's ears were encased in those headphones. And the Colt Python—was that lying around to provide opportunity for an impulse killing? No—that macabre scenario had been meticulously planned. But in that case, why omit so vital a detail as the suicide note—a blunder out of character with the whole operation?

On the desk lay a neat pile of books—each sprouting folded slips of paper which marked pages of reference. I studied the titles. *The Trains Ran On Time* by N. J. Curtois had a dust-jacket embellished with a flattering picture of Benito Mussolini. *Force of Arms*—a standard work on military history by Nigel Mullard—had graced my bookshelf at Oxford fifteen years before. *Urban Guerilla* by Ernst Zuckmayer was much more recent—a blotch-print paperback published in San Francisco by

Liberation International. *Mercenary Achievement* appeared to be the autobiography of one T. Hoskyns-Rider, produced by a vanity-publishing concern in Truro and illustrated with carefully posed photographs of young men sitting in jeeps and lorries or brandishing World War Two weaponry.

Had Garland been working on a new book? I glanced at the sheet of paper in his electric typewriter.

Industrial unrest and recent economic crises in Great Britain have provided both opportunities and stimuli for the establishment of cadres comprising ostensibly public-spirited men (and a few women) whose stated object is the provision of alternative forms of administration and law-enforcement should anarchy threaten. In face of this phenomenon the present generation of politico-economic commentators seems unable to look beyond the so-called Blackshirt rallies of the 1930s and the general strike of 1926, both of which are highly emotive subjects. However, the true historian, oft maligned for his apparent indifference to such political molehills, looks back to that veritable mountain in our national history—the raising and development of the New Model Army under Oliver Cromwell. Nevertheless, the contemporary scene is not without its disquieting aspects . . .

Garland's last word on the subject? Not quite. An audio-stenographer's recorder lay beside the typewriter, its earphones draped over the keyboard. I picked up the grey plastic stethoscope and listened.

The sound of Garland's voice was strangely disturbing. *He, being dead, yet speaketh . . .*

'. . . and in order to obtain a truly balanced view of the situation I shall now consider available evidence relating to private armies, properly so called, in Great Britain.

Resisting the temptation to concentrate on the more heavily publicized and bizarre organizations in Scotland, Wales and Ireland, I shall commence this study within the strict confines of England itself. In nineteen seventy-five there were twenty-three organizations openly recruiting members of both sexes who were invited to regard themselves as fulfilling a function similar to that of the now-defunct Civil Defence Corps. These twenty-three may be considered, without exaggeration, as merely the tip of an iceberg. Typical of the submerged ninety per cent is the Register of Expertise and Advisory Personnel—ostensibly a non-profit-making employment agency. Registered as a charity, it enjoys full tax benefits—'

I switched off—disappointed. That ponderous style might suit an academic reader, but where was the sparkling prose which made Garland's earlier work so popular?

Leaving the house I strolled through the old priory ruins along the path of our flight the previous evening. In the chapel, sun warmed my back and through the western door I could see the tops of trees flanking the stream in its shallow depression beyond. Those old grey stones made a perfect frame for a scene which widened at each step . . .

And as I emerged beneath the arch, a man sprang for cover in the copse below.

CHAPTER SEVEN

'Poacher,' said Ron loftily. 'Checking traps. Watch it, boyo—you'll end up seeing Wright behind every bush.'

I had returned to find him studying TCO files—disgruntled at being roused from slumber to scribble his signature on the courier's receipt pad. Now we were all sprawled about *Plantagent*'s after-deck, discussing our morning's efforts over iced Coke and biscuits.

'Poacher?' I appealed to the others. 'Will you listen to the rural studies expert? D. H. Lawrence rides again—the countryside peopled with tongue-tied yokels whose smouldering eyes lust after the squire's daughter. Meladdo down yonder was different. Natty blazer and all. Anyway, your sort of poacher went out years ago.'

'Like the branch line from Brentwell Junction?' asked Anne innocently. 'We all make mistakes, darling. As for the smouldering eyes—they're still around. That's the way it was this morning in the village store. Half a dozen women holding a regular convention round the bacon-slicer. I went in—*chop!*—conversation went out. They just *stared.*' She wriggled her shoulders at the memory.

'D'you blame 'em?' demanded Ron, holding cupped hands to his eyes and staring at her as through binoculars. '*These yere be zimple country parts, lady. We'm not used to seeing gals in shorts as short as that. Give our menfolk palpitations, they will.*' He turned to me. 'And while your spouse had been demoralizing the local biddies, what about us? Not got very far, have we, matey?

You've stood by and watched the blue people panting after a wild goose. I've been slogging through TCO files. D'you realize, some of them are twenty-five years old? That's going back one hell of a time. Garland brought down more people than I'd realized—plenty with families or friends to even up the score. But would they wait so long? He's been a sitting target here, ten years. Takes a special kind of hate to survive that time. Check the files. I'll lay even money you're none the wiser when you've finished.'

I stared up at the tiller arm silhouetted against the clear blue sky. 'Beth Garland may be able to help. She's home by now, but I'll give her time to adjust to what's happened. Meantime, you can run me over to Brentwell after lunch. I want to see what's at the other end of that railway track.'

The answer—a beautifully preserved Victorian station building. Over the booking-hall entrance a fresh-painted sign proclaimed *WILDE VALLEY RAILWAY —BRENTWELL STATION.*

Of more immediate interest was the board at the gate of the goods yard.

WRIGHT & BABBACOMBE (AGRICULTURAL EQUIPMENT) LIMITED.

As we walked through the booking-hall on to the platform, time retreated before us. A slim green slot machine defied the Trade Descriptions Act by advertising bars of Nestle's Chocolate—1d each. *VIROL* and *STEPHEN'S INK* were extolled from large sheets of enamelled metal bolted to the station walls. Posters abounded. A ruddy-cheeked fisherman leaped at us like an Olympic hurdler—*SKEGNESS IS SO BRACING.*

Young men in Gatsby suits were depicted gazing from carriage windows at lakeland mountains. Vintage cars were being winched aboard the Newhaven-Dieppe ferry.

Fresh ballast had been laid on the old track and from between the platforms twin sets of rails stretched into the distance. Here was a station such as my father would have known as a boy in the twenties.

From the Stationmaster's Office a young man emerged clutching a board on which sexual discrimination was writ large. *LADIES' WAITING ROOM.*

'Not open today,' he said. 'The fun starts on Saturday.'

Ron gazed about with approval. 'What's this, then—the local steam preservation society?'

The young man rested his sign on a venerable bench. 'The Wilde Valley Railway,' he announced proudly. 'At least, it will be when we've finished. Look, if you're really interested I can spare a few minutes to show you round. I'm Michael Babbacombe—for my sins, treasurer of the company.' He coughed. 'Hint hint. All contributions thankfully received.'

I pointed towards the goods yard. 'Wright and Babbacombe?'

'Ah no. I mean—yes.' He laughed. '*Yes*, I'm that Babbacombe. *No*, I'm not treasurer of that company. I meant the railway.'

'Is Colin Wright with you?'

'Old Colin? No, he's not around just now. Oh—you mean is he the Wright of Wright and—? Yes, indeed, he is that. I say—you friends of his?'

I shook my head. 'We're cruising the canals. *Czarina's* moored alongside us.'

He looked at me blankly.

'Your partner's boat.'

'Didn't know he had one—but that's Colin for you. Always on the lookout for a new toy. Now what can I show you? Everything's a bit topsy-turvy right now. Grand opening, Saturday—yet here we are still setting the scene.'

'Very effective.' My appreciation was genuine.

'Think so? But let's do the thing properly. Hang on a moment.' He trotted back to the Stationmaster's Office. Almost immediately we heard distant sounds of an approaching steam train. Babbacombe rejoined us, a smile on his youthful face as the noise grew ever nearer. I could picture a powerful Pacific locomotive hauling laden carriages at full speed. Invisible, it swept through the station, whistle shrieking, pistons thudding, wheels a thunder on the singing rails. So effective was the illusion that I even seemed to catch the half-forgotten smell of mingled smoke and hot oil. Then the monster was past and roaring away into the distance.

Babbacombe grinned. 'There she goes—the old *Flying Scotsman*, brought to you through the miracle of ultraphonic sound. *Sic transit gloria mundi.*'

As he spoke I caught the faraway gasping of another engine.

'Busy line,' I said.

He grinned again. 'We've enough sound effects for a whole day. Colin's idea. Me—I'm just interested in steam. Give me a length of track and an old engine and I'm content. But Colin—he's a stickler for detail. Doesn't know a Gresley from a saddle-tank, but it's thanks to him the Wilde Valley Railway is on the map. So, roll on Saturday when the tape's cut and we're in business. Here—have a leaflet. Tells you all about it. If you're still around at the weekend, come over and join the fun.'

I glanced at the printed sheet out of polite interest.

12.00 NOON—OPENING CEREMONY BY STEPHEN GARLAND, ESQ. OF TONGSTONE PRIORY—HONORARY CHAIRMAN, WVR.

The pounding engine was nearly on us. I tapped the paper. 'You haven't heard?'

My tone brought a wary look to his eyes. 'What's happened?'

I shouted above the thunderous din. 'Stephen Garland shot himself last night.'

Babbacombe looked stunned. His lips shaped themselves into an *O* and I knew he was saying *'Shot?'*—but the word was drowned by a whistle blast shrilling above the roar of steam and steel. In three strides he was across the platform and into the Stationmaster's Office. Another moment and the deafening clamour was snatched away. Silence surged into our battered ears. Babbacombe's footsteps seemed unnaturally loud as he returned.

'Suicide?' He was incredulous. 'Not Garland. Firm as the Rock of Gibraltar. Why in God's name would he kill himself?' There was a long silence, then he ran paint-blotched fingers through his hair. 'This is a blow.' He sounded dazed. 'I don't want to sound callous, but what the hell do we do about Saturday? We can't cancel things at this late stage. I'll have to get busy. Old Colin will know what to do. Where's he moored?'

'Just by Tongstone Priory.'

'Then he knows what's happened?'

'We haven't seen him since last night.' I chose my

words carefully. 'He didn't sleep aboard.'

'He'll be at home. I'd better call him right away. I'm sorry—I didn't ask your name.'

I told him. He nodded and looked at us helplessly. 'D'you mind if we skip the conducted tour? This business about Stephen Garland . . .'

'We'll be on our way.' I glanced over my shoulder. 'Can I get back to Tongstone along the track?'

He hesitated. 'There's no public right of way—but be my guest. The new permanent way only reaches three miles at present. Beyond that it's just how British Rail left it, six years ago. You did mean to walk? I wouldn't advise you to take a car along there.'

Ron said, 'He's walking. You won't catch me risking my springs.'

Babbacombe nodded. 'Wise man. *We* use it, but our stuff's built for rough going like that.'

While Ron drove to Tongstone I trudged beside the newly-laid rails, past sheds filled with agricultural machinery—harvesters . . . giant tractors . . . odd-shaped equipment for uses beyond my knowledge.

Landrovers.

Wright and Babbacombe were in the rental business. A cumbersome combine came roaring out of one of the sheds, rocking and bouncing its way towards Furzeby. Past the goods yard the tracks merged into a single line beside which even the widest farm vehicle might travel freely. That depot could supply equipment for every season of the farmer's year, direct to fields beside the old branch line.

According to Babbacombe's leaflet, the Wilde Valley Railway enthusiasts planned to push their track as far as Furzeby. Reading between the lines—an appropriate exercise in the circumstances—I gathered that the society was far from running out of steam but that cash was low. Hence the festivities arranged for the coming weekend.

Standing on the fresh ballast I gazed along the track. Michael Babbacombe might be a steam fanatic but he had a shrewd eye for business. When that line stretched to Furzeby he would have a smooth delivery service to customers for miles around.

I trudged beside the rust-dull rails, past gradient posts, distance markers and tall poles supporting huge silvered loudspeaker trumpets. At the end of the line stood a set of buffers and beside the track a short wooden platform on brick stilts. *RIVERSIDE HALT*.

At the site of the old level crossing I took to the fields, joining the towpath where the stream flowed under a decaying wooden bridge. On the far bank a morose fisherman watched his motionless float. Trees . . . water . . . and man linked to his primeval past by one nylon umbilical. Constable might have painted the scene. A timeless quality about that angler suggested he had posed for the artist, then stayed on and on, ever hopeful of a bite.

I reached *Plantagenet* to find Ron fuming.

'Trouble. I've just called the office. Someone's made a complete cock-up of things on the other side. Clare's father was supposed to get a message to her school telling them not to worry. The message was sent . . .' He paused and took a deep breath.

I waited. 'And—?'

'And *nothing*. It was never received. Mislaid . . . intercepted—you tell me. All hell's broken loose up in Massachusetts. They think the kid's been snatched. Now everybody's screaming. Police, FBI—the whole damn shooting-match. I *knew* something like this would happen!'

'Poor Daddy,' said Clare quietly.

Ron glared. *'Poor Daddy,'* he echoed bitterly, '—is well out of it. And that's just the trouble. People are asking where he is—and those who know aren't saying. The opposition must be laughing themselves sick. All they have to do is wait. The media are stirring things up. When the news can do most political damage, out it'll come—unless Poor Daddy gets his finger out and pulls off this deal of his, one-time. But God help us all if anybody gets on to you. Young lady, right now you are very hot property. Know what you're holding in your hands? Your father's political future—plus that of your top man. Election year, remember. This little venture could prove the vote-swinger. And *our* involvement could put the skids under Anglo-American relations. So . . .' His finger stabbed home the words. 'When we say "Stay out of sight"—you *stay . . . out . . . of . . . sight*!' He turned to me. 'Wandering along the towpath, she was, when I got here.'

'I was collecting wild flowers,' said Clare hotly. 'What am I supposed to do all day? No television . . . nothing on the radio. I'm *bored*.'

Sullen silence lengthened uncomfortably. We sat there—Ron glowering . . . Clare staring hot-eyed at her clenched hands.

Anne stood up. 'You can all help get the table ready and then we'll have tea, huh?'

Maybe Anglo-American relations had a chance.

* * *

I dialled Babbacombe's number from the village call-box.

'Why hello, Mr Meynell. Found your way back all right then? What can I do for you?'

'I'm worried about your partner's boat. He's left it wide open. Can't find his number in the book.'

I heard his chuckle. 'It's ex-directory—one of Colin's little foibles. But I'm sure he won't mind my giving it to you, under the circumstances. *Brentwell 403*. I've been trying ever since you left, but no joy. If you get through, ask him to call me, will you?'

I had small hope of success but it was worth a try. Wright's phone *burr-burred* at me along the wire from Brentwell. I was about to hang up when the ringing stopped.

'Colin?' A woman. Anxiety and indignation—both were in that shrill voice.

No sense asking if Wright were home. 'David Meynell here. Who's speaking?'

For answer—a click . . . and the dialling tone.

CHAPTER EIGHT

'If you're from the press, the answer's *No*!'

Thus spake the guardian of the Priory—a pert young woman in a green nylon overall. My mental picture of the tyrannical Mrs Frost was all wrong. I expected a grim-faced harridan in black—the sinister housekeeper Hollywood once loved to depict.

I tried again. 'If you'll just tell Mrs Garland, David Meynell's here . . .'

Her eyes narrowed. 'Better come in. Been plagued with newspaper people and other gawpers, we have—ever since she got back.' Stepping aside for me to enter the hall she hurried away without another word, her smart shoes clacking noisily across the flagstones. A minute later she returned.

'She'll see you.' Her tone was unceremonious—even ungracious. 'This way.'

I followed her past the wide stairs to a small parlour bright with warm-rayed evening sun. Beth Garland was seated at a delicate Regency writing-desk. Setting down her pen she rose and came across the room towards me. Now in her mid-thirties she had retained in full measure the disturbing beauty I remembered from her wedding-day, twelve years before. To this, time—for once merciful—had added further gifts of gentle charm and gracious maturity. Her fair hair hung loose and she wore a cool full-length cotton dress of Wedgwood blue and white.

'David! They told me you were in the neighbourhood.

It's good of you to call.'

I took both her outstretched hands and kissed them lightly. They were cool but there was warmth in their grip. 'I'm so sorry.'

She glanced over my shoulder and a frown of annoyance creased the smoothness of her forehead. '*Thank* you, Mrs Frost,' she said with exaggerated emphasis. I heard the door close.

'Come and sit down, David,' We crossed to a window seat and sat in silence for fully a minute. About her clung a delicate perfume which whispered of roses by starlight. She patted my hand gently. 'Bless you—you always had the gift of saying nothing, at the right time. David—what's happened? Have I been completely and utterly blind? Why did Stephen do it?'

'The police—'

She sighed. 'They've been absolutely marvellous—but do they have to be so painfully tactful? There's Sergeant Pollard, still suggesting it could have been an accident. The idea of Stephen having an accident with his revolver is ludicrous. He was far too careful—and he wouldn't dream of tinkering with a gun in the study.'

'The police deal in evidence,' I said cautiously.

'Evidence!' There was abrasive bitterness in her whisper. 'What's that—without an interpreter? The police found Stephen sitting—but you'll know all that. He'd been listening to a record. That's what they told me. *Listening to a record*. Dear God—it could have been *The Sound of Music* for all they cared. When I found out what the record was, I knew it was nonsense to call Stephen's death an accident. He was listening to Mahler's Ninth.'

'That's significant?'

'To me. To anyone who knew how Stephen felt about Mahler. He didn't just *listen*—he *devoured.* Nothing was allowed to distract him. That's why he bought the headphones. He'd shut his eyes and drift off into a private world of his own. Mahler was . . . *special.*' She turned away as though the memory hurt. 'So you see what I mean? It's ridiculous to suggest he was playing around with a revolver while that disc was on the turntable.'

'Beth—just what are you suggesting?'

She stared through the window at the shadowed garden and the old priory beyond. Then she leaned towards me, glancing round as though afraid of being overheard.

'Listen, David—I can't bring myself to tell this to the police, but I've got to talk to someone. The more I think things out, the more convinced I am that Stephen committed suicide. I don't care what the police say—the feeling's there.'

I had hoped for a different answer. 'We saw him, this time yesterday evening, Beth. He gave not the slightest indication of what you're suggesting.'

She looked towards the tall longcase clock near the door. 'Six o'clock?' Her voice was still little more than a whisper. 'Then why did he phone me at half past seven to say he wouldn't be coming up to Glencairn today?'

'You spoke to him?'

'No. We have friends near the hotel where I was staying. I'd gone over there for dinner. Didn't get Stephen's message till I arrived back at the hotel, close on eleven—and before I'd really taken it in, the police were telling me he was dead.'

'Beth, let's be clear about this. It could be important.

When Stephen left us, down at the canal—that would be around seven—he was quite definitely coming to join you, early today. Yet by half past seven he'd changed his mind. Why?'

'I've no idea. According to the girl on the hotel switchboard he didn't give a reason. Mind you, that's typical of Stephen. He hates—hated—passing a personal message through a third party.'

'Then you have nothing to justify your fear that he took his own life.'

Another sigh. 'Put like that—no. But when you've been married to a man for twelve years . . .' She clasped her hands. '*Something's* been worrying him for weeks now—really getting to him. He's been moody . . . withdrawn.'

'What sort of thing? The estate? His writing?'

Her hair swung about her shoulders as she shook her head. 'More . . . personal. But he wouldn't talk about it. He just *brooded*. Then there was the music. He'd sit for hours with those headphones on. David, I've seen tears in his eyes—especially when he was listening to Mahler. I know—that's unbelievable to you. But you only knew Stephen Garland the man of action. He had another side to his nature—sentimental . . . nostalgic. You'd call it weakness, I suppose.'

'Come on, Beth—you know me better than that.'

She patted my hand again. 'Of course. Not you personally—I meant the Department. You know, sometimes I think he even regretted all those years he spent with the Ministry. You two had a lot in common. But I haven't answered your question, have I? All I can say is this—the idea of Stephen sitting in that chair, listening to Mahler and—at the same time—playing around with one of his guns . . . that's *out*. But if things had got on top of him and he'd decided to take his life . . . I can think of no way he'd rather go than listening to that music.'

'Have you told this to the police?'

A faraway look crept to her eyes. 'They haven't asked.'

Before leaving the Priory I took another look round the study. Beth had returned to her letter-writing and I was alone. There on the turntable lay the first movement of the Mahler symphony. The sleeve for a two-record album rested against the side of Garland's chair. Picking it up, I glanced at the printed programme note and read the words of Alban Berg, written more than sixty years earlier.

I see within it the expression of a singular love for this earth, the desire to live there in peace, fully to enjoy nature's abundance—before being surprised by death! For the latter approaches irresistibly . . .

But death had not approached Stephen Garland to the measured strains of Mahler. It had surprised him as he sat listening to Elgar's *Enigma*. So, why the switch? In putting together that grisly tableau, Wright had revealed an artist's delicacy of touch. The Mahler disc had enhanced the illusion just enough to convince Beth.

Michael Babbacombe had called his partner a stickler for detail.

A remarkably well-informed stickler.

As I left the house, the dark blue police van was coming slowly up the drive. Pollard and Redgrave going the rounds of their manor. The sergeant gave a friendly nod.

'Spare a minute, Mr Meynell?'

We took a stroll through the rose garden. The evening air was thick with ladybirds; trees, shrubs and petals appeared blood-spattered wherever the tiny insects settled and folded their crimson wing-cases.

Pollard savoured the roses with a deep breath. 'Marvellous! Look at 'em. Put my humble efforts to shame. You a gardener, Mr Meynell?'

'No opportunity. We live in a flat.'

He shook his head. 'Wouldn't do for me. I've always liked a garden. Even in Africa I managed a patch round the bungalow.' He cleared his throat. 'But I mustn't bore you. I understand you have a colleague with you now. Your people believe in doing things thoroughly.'

'Typical Civil Service carry-on. Everything in duplicate. Actually Metcalfe knew Stephen Garland before I did, and he's still with the same department. That's why he's here. I'm only involved because I happened to be on the spot.'

He nodded. 'Been having a chat with Mrs Garland?'

'Condolences. She's taking it very well.'

'Hmm.' He frowned. 'She's keeping something back. I *know* it.'

'She's convinced it was suicide. Garland phoned her last night at half-seven to say he wasn't going up to Glencairn.'

He stood still. 'Now why the hell couldn't she tell *us* that?'

'Forgot, maybe. It's been a rough day for her. I'd like to know what happened between the time he left our boat and the time he made that call. He told us he was off to Scotland today. Half an hour later, he'd changed his mind.'

Pollard carefully flicked half a dozen ladybirds from his jacket. '*Had* he? If he planned to do away with himself, he'd hardly tell you. Has Mrs Garland come out with any more confidences like that?' He breathed through his nose. 'Sorry if I sound a shade sarcastic, but the way some people carry on, they must reckon we're psychic or something.'

I gave a sympathetic smile. 'That disc on the turntable—she think's it's significant. One of Garland's favourites. Appropriate music for a final curtain.'

He snorted impatiently. 'Woman's intuition! The coroner'll make short work of that. I'd better have another word with her.'

'I'd rather you didn't mention what I've told you.'

'Don't want to dry up the wells of confidence, eh? Okay—I'll wait till morning, anyway. Give her time to think things over. Guilt-complex—that's her trouble, if you ask me. Doesn't want to admit her husband killed himself in case folk say she failed him. I've seen it before.'

When the blue van had gone I walked slowly across the parched lawn to the ruins of the old Gilbertine priory. That brief conversation had been an effort—so much I could say . . . so little I dared.

Passing through the remains of the canons' infirmary I entered the cloister, pacing flagstones once familiar to meditating religious. Long centuries of neglect had left that pavement cracked and uneven. My rubber-soled deckshoes made no sound as I trod carefully to avoid grass-tufted crevices. At the corner by the sacristy I turned west, head bowed against the glare of the setting sun. Thirty paces then left again towards the tumbled walls of refectory and parlour.

Peace and holy calm . . .

. . . rudely shattered by a muttered obscenity wafted to my ears from the chapel. Not—I ventured to think—an echo from the past. Bow Street's argot for unlawful carnal knowledge would not be numbered among the old monks' vocabulary.

Turning, I hurried through the canons' day door into the chapel. On the base of a pillar sat a youth, nursing his ankle. Dark blue blazer . . . grey flannels . . . neatly brushed short hair—he seemed to have strayed thither from the nineteen fifties. Only the mark on his right wrist was out of character. As he massaged his ankle the cuff of his blazer rode up to reveal a pink and blue tattooed crucifix. I recognized the man who had ducked out of sight in the copse that morning.

Catching sight of me he struggled to his feet. 'Mr Meynell?'

I nodded. 'Have you been following me, lad?'

'Not *following*, sir—just waiting for a chance to speak to you. Saw you were busy with Sergeant Pollard just now.'

'What's wrong with your ankle?'

'Twisted it.'

I looked at him, hard. 'Okay—I'm here. What d'you want to say?'

He took a deep breath. 'Colonel Garland's compliments, sir, and will you join him at the Lodge?'

The polite formality of his invitation sounded quaint. I had not been addressed in that way for years. *Colonel*? That must be Andrew, Stephen Garland's brother—lieutenant (acting captain) when the British army kicked him out.

'Right now?'

The youngster nodded earnestly. 'If convenient, sir. The Colonel wishes to discuss a matter of importance.'

There could only be one matter important enough to justify such persistence.

'Lead on.'

He led—limping heavily. Leaving the ruined chapel by the west door, we trudged along a sunken lane between high hedges which screened us from the house. After a hundred yards it passed the end of a rutted track leading across a paddock towards the stable block. I heard the clock on the coach-house strike the half hour. Six-thirty.

'You work for Andrew Garland?' I asked.

'Alex Howell, the colonel's secretary-cum-chauffeur-cum . . . well, you name it. Believe me, it's a full life. Being crippled the way he is only makes him drive himself harder. Do you know him, sir?'

'Only by repute.'

'A great man.'

I smiled. 'There aren't many about.'

The lane entered a thick copse and immediately the air grew cooler. In contrast to the well-tended Priory estate, this dark wood had reverted to nature. Splintered branches lay on the ground or hung from ravaged trunks like broken limbs. Here and there trees had been torn up by the roots to lean drunkenly against their neighbours. The place was dark and vaguely sinister as we moved further into its depths.

The Lodge matched its gloomy setting to perfection. Its name conjured the Bavarian hunting-lodge of romance—but reality was no more than a pair of estate workers' cottages knocked into one. Tangled bushes and undergrowth smothered a tiny garden and wild briars clawed the lower windows—alien invaders seeking entrance. A rotting wooden garden gate sagged open and green moss carpeted the crumbling brick path.

Beyond the threshold—a cramped hall, lit only by one narrow window halfway up a tiny stair. The young man touched a switch and cold fluorescence flooded the little vestibule. Polished linoleum . . . distempered walls . . . typed notices pinned to a board . . . conical fire extinguisher . . . red buckets filled with sand—all struck a chord in my memory. Even the smell of floor polish was familiar—the atmosphere of dingy efficiency breathed daily by minions at the Ministry.

A nameboard screwed to one of the doors completed the picture.

COL. GARLAND.

I was ushered into a tiny office bearing superficial resemblance to my Director's room at Whitehall. A paperback edition of a leather-bound original. The wall panelling was wood-effect paper; imitation grained hide covered a meagre desk and the battered filing cabinets were of redundant design.

Alex Howell pointed to a ruptured replica Windsor chair. 'Colonel Garland won't keep you long, sir.'

When he had gone I sat uncomfortably and took in my surroundings. Theatrical—a room assembled for effect. The door opened and the illusion was complete. In shabby blazer and fawn slacks, with striped cravat overflowing his check open-neck shirt. Andrew Garland was the stage archetype of a senior army officer. Lean face . . . high cheekbones . . . clipped moustache . . . thinning hair plastered close to his skull—every detail was correct. He walked stiffly as if each step demanded concentrated effort. Crippled? I recognized something else—the over-careful gait of an unconfessed alcoholic desperately compensating to conceal his problem.

'Ha! Meynell.' A high-pitched bark. Without another word he tottered past me and lowered himself awkwardly into a swivel chair behind the desk.

'Mr Garland?' He'd get no 'colonel' from me. 'Your secretary tells me you have something important to discuss. I'm investigating your brother's death. Is that what you want to see me about?'

'Ha!' Lifting a pipe from the desk he flicked a lighter and sucked flame into the charred briar bowl. Then he fanned away the smoke and stared at me with cold blue eyes. 'Feeling pleased with yourself?'

'Should I be?'

'Ha! Well—come to think of it—*no*. Right now you have little cause for self-congratulation. That's the price of over-confidence.'

I glanced at my watch. Anne would be preparing dinner. 'Can we get to the point?'

'Ha! The *point*, as you call it, is very simple—a matter of untimely death.'

'Your brother's?'

He took the pipe from his mouth and pointed the stem at me.

'*Yours*,' he said.

CHAPTER NINE

'I have a reputation to maintain.' He shifted his position in the swivel chair, wincing as he did so. 'In my time I've ordered forty-five executions. Seventeen I carried out myself. Seventeen. The experience taught me one thing. If a man's to be done to death, he deserves to know why.' His eyes narrowed. 'Tell me, Meynell—did my brother know?'

'How can I answer a question like that?'

A sigh of irritation whistled in his nose. 'Don't try my patience. I know you were there. I know *why* you were there. All I'm asking is, did *Stephen* know? Good God, man—it's a simple enough question.'

I stood up. 'And one I don't choose to answer. Listen, Garland—I know about you. You may have promoted yourself banana republic colonel, but when we kicked you out you had two pips on your shoulder—and you weren't even fit to wear those. Thirty years you've been playing soldiers and now the game's over. If you've anything worth saying, I'll listen. If not—' I walked towards the door.

'Meynell!' His voice was almost a whisper. I looked over my shoulder, straight into the line of fire of a Colt Python—twin to the one I had seen in Wright's hand. Garland's prominent Adam's apple bobbed up and down as he swallowed noisily. 'Don't push your luck. In my book a condemned man is allowed certain privileges, so we'll overlook that childish outburst. Sit down.'

I sat—quickly. 'Put the gun away, Garland. You're not in the jungle now. Pull that trigger and you're finished.'

Puckered lids flickered over his watery eyes. 'I'm finished already. The game's over. Isn't that what you said? Think I care what happens to me?'

He set the gun on the desk but kept one hand on it. 'Thirty years I've been fighting other people's wars. You know your Housman? *What God abandoned, these defended, and saved the sum of things, for pay.* But not just for pay. I'd never take up arms for a cause I didn't believe in. And the best cause of all was England. I used to dream of coming back here . . . settling down . . . living the life of a gentleman in the only place on God's earth where a gentleman can live. Most of my contemporaries have done all right for themselves. Grown fat while I was sweating it out. Now I wanted my slice of the cake. Then . . . Ha! First time I ever jumped by parachute. Landed badly. End of my soldiering. Damn near the end of me. Takes me all my time to hobble this far every morning. So I came home. *Home?* The place is bankrupt—economically . . . morally . . . spiritually. My savings—well, you know what's happened to the pound. And as for standards of decency. Ha! You've all been wallowing in filth so long you've grown used to the stink.'

'What has all this to do with me?'

'Ha! Just the sort of remark I'd expect. You're conditioned—like the rest of your generation. Blind to what's going on around you. And you see the result? My brother had the guts to speak out—to tell people how rotten the system is—and what happened? He got a visit from one of your lackeys. Threats, Meynell—threats!

Did you really think a Garland would back down just because some pasty-faced kid came tut-tutting round his door? Your fat boss knew better than that. So he sent you. Yes—he'd find that amusing. Stephen *liked* you—really thought you were different from the others. He was looking forward to your visit, last night.'

'You think I killed him?'

'Think. I *know*. I left the Priory at a quarter past eight last night. You were due at half past. I phoned him just after the half hour. No reply.'

'He was already dead.'

His bleary eyes widened in feigned surprise. 'What a brilliant fellow you are, to be sure. The police couldn't be anything like as precise as that. But then—they're at a disadvantage, aren't they? Poor old Pollard doesn't even know you were at the Priory last night.'

I leaned forward in my chair. Immediately, the revolver was in his hand and pointing at my stomach. I waved it away. 'Finished? Right—now let's just put the record straight and I can get back to my dinner. *Yes*, I was at the Priory last night. *Yes*, I didn't tell the police—because that would compromise one of our operations which has nothing to do with your brother. But *no*—I didn't kill Stephen. He was already dead when I arrived.'

He shook his head in disbelief. 'Eight-fifteen he was full of the joys of spring . . . telling me about his plans for the future. Ten minutes later—pouf!—suicide. That what you're telling me? You must think I'm a simpleton!'

'Your brother was murdered—and I know who did it.'

A sneer tilted his moustache. 'But you can't tell the

police because it might compromise your department. Yet you tell *me*. Why?'

'You're holding a gun.'

'Ha! And this mysterious man who shot my brother—'

'Colin Wright.'

He burst into genuine laughter. '*Wright*? That bladder of lard! Why on earth would he want to kill Stephen? Let's ask him, shall we?'

His left hand reached for a red phone on his desk.

'Alex? Get me Colin Wright, will you? . . . Hmm? . . . Well, try him at home, anyway.' He put down the phone and looked at me. 'Ha! I wondered how you came to pull his name out of the hat. You've met him, of course. His boat's tied up alongside yours.'

'But he's not aboard—and you won't find him at home, either.'

'That proves something?'

'He's on the run.'

The fingers of Garland's left hand beat an impatient tattoo on the silent phone. 'You actually saw him shoot Stephen?'

'No—it happened a minute or two before I arrived. He hadn't started to fake the suicide.'

He tugged his moustache thoughtfully. 'I see. You interrupted him.'

'I suppose so. We got out through the study window.'

'*We*?'

'My wife and I. Wright took a shot at us while we were in the old priory ruins but we got away.'

'Oh, bravo! Keep it up, Meynell. A thrill a minute. But—let me see—he knew you'd seen him, so that's why he's on the run. There now—am I right?'

At last. I leaned back, confident I had got through to his muddled brain.

He smiled. 'You're not only a liar, Meynell—you're a damned poor liar. First you expect me to believe Colin Wright killed my brother. Then you say he knows you spotted him. Right?'

'Right.'

His moist eyes were alight with triumph. 'Then why in God's name did he waste time setting everything up to look like suicide. He'd get away from the Priory like a bat out of hell. No, my friend—you'll have to do better than that!'

I was working on it when the phone rang. My inquisitor lifted the handset.

'Yes Alex? . . . Yes . . . *Is* she? . . . And she's tried—? . . . I see. Right . . . No—that won't be necessary.'

Uncertainty puckered his forehead as he looked at me. 'The gods are kind to you, Meynell. Wright's not at home, but his girlfriend is. Sandra Howell—my secretary's sister. She spent last night at Wright's place, but he didn't show up. She's heard nothing from him since midday yesterday.'

I stood up. He made no move. '*Now* do you believe me?' I demanded.

'Let's just say I suspend judgement. The court grants stay of execution. Think yourself lucky—and get out. Oh—and, Meynell—don't go whining to the police about my threatening behaviour. It's your word against mine. Somehow I don't think they'll rate your honesty very high if they learn you were at the Priory last night.'

At dinner aboard *Plantagenet* I described my meeting with Beth but said nothing about the Lodge and its embittered tenant. Ron had met Sergeant Pollard in the village and taken the opportunity to present his credentials.

'Can't say he's exactly overwhelmed at the prospect of having the Department's best brains on his patch. More *resigned,* like.' He attacked his steak. 'Mmm—and he's decidedly peeved about the way Beth Garland's behaving. Not bothered about all the heavy psychological bit with that Mahler record—but he reckons she should have told him about the phone call. Mmm—could it have been Garland, d'you reckon?'

I jerked a thumb in the direction of *Czarina*. 'Wright has a radio phone.'

Later, the two of us walked in the gathering dusk and I told Ron about Andrew Garland. 'A pathetic has-been, playing president of a court-martial. The performance had its moments—but I couldn't take it seriously.'

He did not share my amusement. 'Let me tell you about this has-been, boyo. Seven fullscale massacres—that's his official record according to our files. God knows what the unofficial score is. And as for courts-martial—he used to boast he only brought guilty men to trial. Prosecutor . . . judge . . . executioner—he was all three rolled into one. He wasn't kidding about those forty-five executions. If anything, he was being modest.'

We reached the wooden bridge over the stream and stood staring down at the first stars reflected in the sluggish waters.

'And now he's just a disillusioned old soak without a pension,' I said. 'I feel sorry for him.'

'Don't. He's poison. All the more dangerous because he's here in England—not up the jungle. Ever heard of reap?'

I looked at him blankly.

'Reap,' he repeated. 'R-E-A-P. Full title, the *Register of Expertise and Advisory Personnel.*'

'Oh *that*. Stephen Garland was going to mention it in his next book.'

'Was he indeed?' Ron tossed a Rennie wrapper into the water and watched it drift slowly away. 'Now that's *very* interesting. Let me tell you about REAP. It has a perfectly respectable front—a legitimate employment agency for redundant executives . . . retired military types . . . pensioned-off pilots. Actually registered as a charity. All subscribers sign a tax covenant, so *REAP* lives up to its name—it harvests the Chancellor's concessions. In fact the whole set-up is a bridge of ultra-right-wing opportunists, pledged to maintain law and order if British administration break down—something they pray for night and day. They just can't wait to bring in their own brand of *top'em and flog'em* justice.'

'And Andrew Garland?'

'Heavily involved with what they call *survival training*. You can guess what that means. So next time he asks you round for a chat, treat it like you would an invitation to supper with the Borgias.'

FRIDAY JULY 16. Morning mist clung to the canal and drifted among overhanging branches as *Plantagenet* moved stern-first downstream to Tongstone Lock. With four people aboard, our reserves of water had dwindled and it was time to replenish the large tank in the narrow-boat's bows. On our waterways map a blue *W* indicated a water point beside the lock cottage.

We moored close to the top gates and Anne jumped ashore to couple our long hose to a dripping tap by the cottage door. In bygone days that tap must have irritated generations of canalside housewives. Boatmen using it found themselves staring directly through the window of the tiny room which served as kitchen, dining room and bathroom. I imagined net curtain stretched defiantly across the glass to preserve a pathetic vestige of privacy.

Or was I wrong? Privacy—like piped water—is a modern luxury. Should I picture that window opened wide—the housewife pausing for a friendly chat with water-folk whose passing brought welcome relief from daily chores. And those same water-folk probably took their water straight from the Cut.

Certainly the present tenants of the cottage encouraged visitors to stand and stare. The little house was home for a young couple—artists who spent their days painting local scenes and embellishing *canalia* with traditional designs of roses and castles. By *canalia* they meant those metal cans, jugs and water-dippers which for the past two centuries have graced cabins and decks aboard working narrow-boats. Examples of their artistry now filled the window—ranged on shelves and hanging from hooks and cords.

Eight-thirty—and the couple were already at work. Beside the water-filled lock the husband in paint-stained shirt and jeans was capturing morning mist on canvas. In the cottage his wife's deft brush-strokes brought full-blown roses to life on a spouted water can.

Plantagenet's diesel thumped evenly, recharging our vital batteries.

Leaning against a doorpost, Ron watched the girl as she bent over her work.

'Business good?'

She nodded without taking her eyes from the can. 'It pays the rent.'

'Closing the locks can't have helped.'

She put the finishing touch to a rose and leaned back, regarding it critically. 'Hasn't hit us yet. We're still working on orders we took days ago. Trouble's going to be when the customers want to collect. Usually they order when they pass through on the outward run, then pick up the stuff on the way back.'

'You don't sell straight off the shelf?'

'Oh sure—but folk like the name of their boat on things. That takes time.' She indicated a pair of newly-decorated locker doors propped against a wall. 'Can we interest you in anything?'

'I'll look around.' Ron stepped into the cottage.

Brush poised, the artist stared after him, disapproval in his eyes. I strolled across for a closer look at his work.

Unfinished, the picture yet held delicacy which lifted it far above the garish daubs I had seen in other makeshift studios along the Cut. There on the canvas, sunlight struggled with wreathing mist adrift among stereoscopic branches.

'For sale?' I asked on impulse.

'Could be.' His voice lacked enthusiasm. 'Depends how I feel when I've finished.'

I left him to his work and perched myself on a worn wooden bollard. A throaty tractor roared over the humped bridge above the lock, spattering the morning air with diesel smoke.

The artist spoke again. 'I have this rule. No haggling over unfinished work.'

'People try to beat you down?'

'Huh!' He wiped his brush on what was once a handkerchief. 'You'd be surprised.'

'But you accept commissions?'

'Occasionally. With most people, it's impulse buying. You may find this hard to believe, but from this rural backwater, my work goes all over the world.' He chuckled. 'Who knows? Some day the Wilde valley may be as well-known on canvas as Dedham Vale.'

'I wish you luck. The country round here certainly has a feel of Constable about it. You've caught it in that picture. So—you're in export. That's where the money is, these days.'

He grinned ruefully. 'Not for me. My overseas buyers come from the American base at Furzeby, up the road—and they pay the going rate for a canvas. But I know for a fact one of my landscapes fetched four hundred dollars in the States, earlier this year. Believe me, that is *not* the going rate over here.'

'*A prophet is without honour in his own country.*'

He waved a reproving brush at me. 'I'll have you know I painted the sign outside the *Haywain*. There's glory for you! *And* a portrait of the squire.'

'Stephen Garland?'

He looked embarrassed. 'You know him? Trust me to open my big mouth too wide. Look—forget I mentioned that portrait, will you? It's rather a delicate matter.'

'Haven't you heard? Garland's dead.'

He turned sharply. 'Dead? No, I had *not* heard. What happened?'

'He shot himself.' I waited for the protest . . . the incredulity.

The artist stared sadly along the mist canal. 'So soon?' he said.

CHAPTER TEN

I stood beside Anne as she steered *Plantagenet* towards our mooring.

'But what did he mean?' she asked. 'You make it sound like he *expected* Stephen to commit suicide.'

'That's exactly how it sounded—but when I asked him, he clammed up. Mumbled something about an artist being father-confessor to his sitter.'

Rounding the bend below the Priory we saw a figure on the towpath beside *Czarina*. For one tense moment I thought—*Wright*? Binoculars gave the reassuring truth—Beth Garland, in jeans and fisherman's sweater, shielding her eyes against the morning sun which was driving the mist from the canal. She moved along to our mooring-place and stood waiting to take our rope.

'David—I was afraid you'd gone.'

'Only as far as the lock. We needed water. I've been chatting with the neighbourhood artist.'

'Brendan?' For a second she looked surprised—almost anxious. 'He's an odd character. Doesn't exactly fit in, around here—if you know what I mean.'

'He's good.'

'I wouldn't know about that. Can we talk? I need advice.'

It took only a couple of minutes to secure the boat, bow and stern. I saw Anne hurrying below and knew she was getting Clare out of sight in the forward cabin.

Moments later the gangplank was out and I was helping Beth aboard.

Introductions . . . condolences . . . then—awkward silence. Ron turned to leave but Beth laid a hand on his arm.

'Don't go—please. I'd welcome your opinion. You too, Anne.' She held up a pale blue envelope and slowly drew out the letter it contained. 'This arrived an hour ago in the morning mail. It's from Stephen. He sent it a couple of days ago. It must have got to Glencairn yesterday morning and the hotel forwarded it straight away. Look, you can see the postmarks.'

I took the envelope. The dates checked and the handwriting certainly looked like Stephen Garland's antiquated scrawl.

Beth glanced at the letter and shook her head sadly. 'I just don't know what to do. Remember what I said last night, David? How I had this feeling Stephen's death was no accident?' She sighed. 'I was right. It's all here. Oh God—how can you live with somebody and not notice things? I *knew* something was wrong, but I never dreamed . . . David—he was going blind. *Blind*—the one thing he dreaded. He was such an active man. The thought of being dependent . . .'

I pointed to the letter. 'He actually says he intended taking his own life?'

She nodded miserably. 'While I was away at Glencairn. He didn't want me to be the one who found him. And he asks me to apologize to everybody for the trouble he knew he would cause—and to say he was sorry he couldn't write to all of them individually. He mentions you, David—and the Department. It's a perfectly calm, rational letter. But—what am I to do?'

I turned to stare out of the window. She was being deceived by a cruel and clever forgery—of that I had no doubt. This was no formal suicide note addressed to the coroner. It was a personal letter to the dead man's wife—couched in terms she must recognize and containing authentic detail. But how could Colin Wright know about Garland's association with me and the Department? A new suspicion grew in my mind.

'Have you told anyone else about this?'

'I was going to show it to Andrew—Stephen's brother.'

'I shouldn't do that. Take it straight to the police.'

I caught Ron's frown of disapproval, but I knew what I was saying. The police would run a thorough check on the letter and once they established it as a forgery their enquiry would become what Anne called a whole new ballgame. Wright's disappearance would become significant and the hunt would be on. The man had overreached himself.

Beth was clutching the letter tightly. 'But it's private . . . personal.'

Anne touched her arm. 'Stephen's death isn't a private matter,' she said quietly. 'And how about those farewell messages? If you tell his friends, you might as well tell the police.'

Beth's face was taut with indecision. She thrust the letter deep into a pocket of her jeans. 'I'll think about it. Please—don't say anything about this. I want to do the right thing.'

Sergeant Pollard's words came back to me. *Guilt-complex—that's her trouble.*

* * *

We stood on deck watching her cross the meadows towards the Priory—a lonely figure with shoulders hunched as though battling against an arctic gale.

Ron sucked at his teeth. 'Missed your chance there, boyo. Should have grabbed that letter. It may fool a woman who's just been knocked sideways by her husband's death but it won't fool our gnomes over on Millbank. Not when they check it against Garland's hand written reports.'

I led the way below to where Clare was preparing belated breakfast.

'We haven't done so badly,' I said. The pale blue envelope still lay on the table.

Ron shuffled forward, arms outstretched like Frankenstein's monster. 'Gimme gimme,' he croaked gleefully. 'I'll get that down to London just as soon as the pangs of hunger are assuaged.'

I grabbed the envelope before he could reach it. 'Wright wasn't working alone. Whoever put that letter together knows one hell of a lot about Garland's affairs. Now, who's close to Garland . . . knows his life story from A to Z—and is unscrupulous enough to set up a killing?'

Ron held up his hands as though framing a picture. 'These tired old eyes recognize the identikit. Let's call on the colonel and point out the errors of his ways.'

Screened by trees and scrub we made a circuit of the Lodge. From the rear a broad cinder track led towards the Furzeby road, less than a hundred yards away.

'Should have brought the car,' murmured Ron. 'This is an in-out-and-away operation.'

I nodded. 'I don't fancy dodging about among these

trees while Garland takes potshots from the house.'

'Rest easy, boyo. By the time we've finished he won't be in any mood for that sort of thing.' He clenched his fist and blew on his knuckles in gleeful anticipation.

'Just remember what you told me. He's dangerous and he's on familiar ground. That gives him the advantage.'

'I'll remember. Come on.'

We walked briskly up to the back door. In answer to my knock it was opened by a bony woman with a harrassed expression.

'Yerse?'

Ron beamed at her and consulted a scrap of papaer. 'Morning, love. Name of Garland?'

'Yerse.'

'Lovely. One grand piano and stool, as per order. Okay if we back the van up and bring it through here?'

She stared. 'Grand piano? You're never bringing no grand piano through here! Why—there's not a room in the house as'd take a grand piano. You must'a made a mistake. It's Garland over at the Priory as you're wanting.'

He looked at the paper again. 'Says here *Mr A. Garland—The Lodge—Tongstone*.'

'It's a mistake,' she repeated, less confidently. 'You'll have to take it back.'

'*Take it back*? Do us a favour, love. We come all the way from London. Your Mr Garland in?'

Her face cleared. 'Yerse—you have a word with him. He'll soon sort you out. Grand piano indeed! Come on through, the pair of you.'

We followed her through a kitchen and down a short passage to the hall. She knocked on Garland's door, opened it slightly and poked her head into the room.

'Can you talk to these men, Mr Garland? Wanting to bring a grand piano through my kitchen they are—if you ever heard such foolishness.'

'What?'

Withdrawing hurriedly she turned to Ron. 'Tell him yourself.'

A moment later we were past her and into the room, with the door closed behind us. Before Garland could recover from his surprise Ron had dragged the 38 Special from its holster.

'Hands on the desk, Garland,' he whispered. 'Don't speak. Don't move. Don't even breathe.'

Sliding his left hand along the phone lead he ripped it from the wall. Then he wrenched open the desk drawers one by one, scattering their contents on the floor. I watched him stoop cautiously—covering Garland all the time—and pick the Colt Python from a carpet of typewritten pages.

'Catch!' The gun sailed through the air. My bandaged hands caught it clumsily.

And then—like the wrath of God—my Rennie-sucking colleague moved swiftly round that tiny room and proceeded to wreak systematic havoc. I was totally unprepared for this, but Ron was a seasoned professional in whose madness there was always method and reason. Hypnotized, I watched him deftly twitch a picture from the wall, rest it against the desk and put his foot through glass and canvas. He tilted a laden bookcase until a hundred volumes hit the floor and were kicked savagely into the four corners of the room. From the mantelpiece he lifted a porcelain statuette of a Napoleonic dragoon, weighing it for a moment as though to assess its value. I saw Garland wince as Ron's arm came down like a flail, shattering horse and rider against the desk so that brittle wreckage tumbled into Garland's lap.

Thirty seconds—and the room was transformed into chaos.

'Like you said, boyo—he's on familiar ground.' Ron surveyed the havoc he had created. 'Or rather— he *was*.'

'Why?' choked Garland—his face the colour of creamed mushrooms, his whole body trembling.

Ron looked him over in digust. 'Courtesy. Always talk to a man in the language he understands. Take a good look, friend. I can be much more eloquent if I put my mind to it. The name is Metcalfe. Remember that. won't you? This—' He pointed to the wreckage. '—is my calling card. A gentle hint not to threaten our personnel. In the far corner—David Meynell. You've met. Yesterday you pulled a gun on him, you silly little man, and asked him a lot of questions. Today, he's asking the questions—you're giving the answers . . . or *I* kick your rotten vertebrae out of alignment, disc by disc. You have my word on that.' He looked at me and gestured towards the dazed man. 'All yours boyo.'

I thrust the pale blue envelope in front of Garland's angry eyes. 'Recognise this?'

'I think so.'

'Only *think*?'

He cleared his throat. 'What am I supposed to say? It's my brother's handwriting. First Class mail. Posted in Tongstone on the thirteenth. Addressed to Beth at the Clansman Hotel, Glencairn. Re-addressed and sent on to the Priory yesterday. That satisfy you?'

'You're sure the handwriting's genuine?'

He peered more closely at the envelope. 'I'm sure.'

'Even if I tell you it contained your brother's suicide note?'

'Huh!'

'He couldn't face the prospect of going blind.'

'*My God!*' He was genuinely shaken—or a consummate actor.

'You believe that?' I asked.

'I . . . listen—Stephen had been having trouble with his eyes for a while. Blurred vision . . . blinding headaches. About a month ago he saw a specialist. Brain tumour—affecting the optic nerve. An operation might save his life but would almost certainly destroy his sight. He asked me over to the Priory the other evening to tell me he was going into hospital as soon as he got back from Scotland. That was the first I knew of his trouble. He hadn't told a soul. But he needed to discuss plans for the future. He was quite calm . . . very matter-of-fact. Just what you'd expect of Stephen. I don't know what's in this letter you're talking about—but if it says he was going to kill himself, it's a forgery.'

I held up the envelope again. 'You've just told me this handwriting's genuine. Would you swear to that at the inquest?'

'What would that prove? It's the letter that counts. Now if I saw *that* . . .' He looked at the envelope again and frowned. 'Is it typed or handwritten?' 'The letter? I don't know. Why?'

'Ha! So you haven't seen it. There's a lot you don't know, Meynell. Suppose we stop behaving like savages. If I've misjudged you . . .' He shook his head mournfully as he gazed round the room. 'You've pointed out my error. Now let's conduct the rest of these proceedings under a flag of truce, eh?'

I rested Garland's revolver on the bookcase while Ron slipped the Smith and Wesson out of sight, perched himself on the edge of Garland's desk and sat staring at the sheets of paper scattered beneath his feet.

'Tell us what we don't know,' he said encouragingly.

The older man moved painfully in his chair. 'My brother hasn't written a letter for ages. Not *written.* Arthritis. Used to bring on writer's cramp. He always typed his correspondence. In fact recently, young Alex has done most of that. I've let him spend an hour or so there, most days. That's what's odd about this envelope. You asked if I recognised it. I do. It's hand-made hammered bond, or whatever fancy name they give the stuff. Part of a box of headed stationery I bought Stephen a couple of years back. Christmas present—all used up within six months. He wrote that address all right—but he must have done it over a year ago.'

'And kept the envelope?' I suggested.

'Not Stephen. If he wrote that envelope and didn't need it—straight into the wastepaper basket.' He pinched his lower lip thoughtfully. 'Where somebody found it. You still suspect young Wright?'

'Of the murder—yes. But who's behind him. Who knows enough to put that letter together?'

He stroked his moustache. '*I* had nothing to do with it, if that's what you're suggesting. But if that letter's produced at the inquest, there'll be expert medical witnesses to support what it says about Stephen going blind. The question is, who wanted my brother out of the way?'

Ron unwrapped a Rennie and slipped it into his mouth. 'Who stands to benefit?'

'Ha! Don't look at me. The estate's not entailed—and

I sold my birthright for a mess of pottage years ago—with damn-all to show for it now. I'm only here on sufferance. If I know Beth, she'll have me out on my neck and the Priory turned into a tourist hotel within a year. She's talked enough about the idea—now she's free to do what she wants.' He gave a short humourless laugh. 'There's your answer, Metcalfe. Who stands to benefit? *The widow-woman!*'

CHAPTER ELEVEN

Thick smoke billowed across the Furzeby road as we headed back to Tongstone and the canal. To our right, fire crept across the fields like the battle-lines of mediaeval legend, burning stubble in preparation for autumn ploughing. Here and there, points of flame waved like rallying banners in the midst of an armoured mêlée. I strode angrily through the grey swirl with Ron coughing and spluttering behind me.

'Be reasonable, boyo,' he pleaded. 'He's biased, he's bitter—but he knows Beth Garland better than you do. Suppose there's something between her and Wright—there's a motive for wanting her husband out of the way.'

I rubbed smarting eyes. 'Rubbish. If she's playing around with Wright, she could have walked out on her husband any day. Killing him would be pointless.'

We emerged from the clinging smoke and there ahead of us lay Tongstone—morning sunlight glinting on the gilded weathercock above the church tower.

'You're forgetting the tourist hotel idea,' Ron persisted. 'She'd kiss that goodbye if she walked out on her old man. This way she gets the best of both worlds. At least admit the *possibility*. She could provide facts for the phoney letter. And that's another thing. All we've actually *seen* is the envelope, conveniently left lying around for us to check out. Your face—when Andrew Garland asked if the letter was typed or written! She's conned us, cocko.'

I stopped and faced him. 'All right . . . all right—she's

been cheating on her husband . . . she's persuaded Wright to murder him so she can turn the Priory into an hotel . . . and she's cooked up a fake suicide note. That's what you're asking me to believe? Then answer me this: if she's gone to so much trouble in preparing false evidence, why hasn't she gone straight to the police? You heard what she said. She asked us not to tell anyone about the letter.'

He sighed heavily, taking my arm in fatherly fashion and leading me down the road. 'There are times, friend, when your wide-eyed innocence sets fair to send me *bananas*! She knows we're in with the blue people. Don't you see? She's feeding them information through us. She *wants* them to know. All this coy *Don't tell a soul* routine is eyewash. A show of reticence can be very effective. Ask any stripper.'

At the canal bridge we were about to descend a flight of worn steps to the towpath when the artist hailed us from across the lock.

'Thirty pounds!'

Ron turned to me. 'What's he on about?'

We clambered over the lock gates and joined the painter as he sat putting finishing touches to another canvas—a solitary angler beside the tree-lined canal. I recognized the scene. His easel must have been set up close to where *Plantagenet* now lay.

'The perfect model,' he said, pointing to the fisherman. 'Sat like that for hours.' I studied the picture. 'Looks like the chap I saw yesterday, up by the Priory.'

'Quite likely. Joe Ferstein. He's a major in the US Air Force. This canvas is for him.' He set down his brush and stood up. 'That picture you were asking about. It's finished. Thirty pounds—if you're still interested.'

'I'd like to see it.'

'Hang about.' Massaging his stiffened neck muscles he sauntered into the cottage. A moment later he was back. 'There!'

His pride was justified. Water and mist blended in gentle motion on the still canvas. For a full minute all other thoughts were banished by that pictured perfection.

'You'll take a cheque?' My question sounded irreverent.

He hesitated. 'No possibility of cash, I suppose? We're rather hoping to eat, this weekend.'

'Sorry—I don't have that much on me.'

'Ah well—at least it's not a Diners Club card. I've been offered one of those before now.' He grinned. 'Sure—a cheque will be fine.'

'Can I take the picture right now?'

'Up to you. Normally I'd varnish it after about a week. Could frame it, if that's what you want. Cost extra, of course. Do you a decent frame for a fiver.' He looked at me hopefully.

I tugged my wallet from a hip pocket. 'Cash in advance for the frame—a cheque for the canvas. Fair enough?' That brought a smile to his face.

His receipt was headed *BRENDAN AND MARGERY LAMPE*. With my money in his pocket he was more at ease.

'Hope these water restrictions aren't spoiling your holiday.'

I folded the receipt and slipped it into my wallet. 'Stephen Garland's death has done that. We're investigating it.'

He looked at each of us a shade apprehensively. 'You're police?'

'Defence Ministry. Garland worked for us.'

'Sounds a bit cloak-and-daggerish. Can't say I'm surprised.'

Ron unwrapped a Rennie. 'Nothing seems to surprise you, friend. Last time we were here, you weren't surprised Garland had shot himself.'

Brendan Lampe sat down at his easel and began toying with a brush. 'Know my trouble? I talk too much. If I gave the impression I expected him to blow his brains out, I'm sorry. It wasn't that way at all. Look—I paint portraits. I don't just reproduce what's on the surface. A camera can do that. I go deeper. Some of my esteemed patrons can't take that. They don't like their souls laid bare on canvas.' He began idly brushing burnt umber onto his thumbnail. 'What did I see in Garland? A man with precious few inner resources. Superficially a man of action—like his brother. You know our local ex-mercenary? The fighting's over for him, but soldiering's a drug and he's hooked. What he's up to is nobody's business, but I tell you, there are some rum goings-on in the woods round his place. You'll find a dozen or so great hulking yobbos under canvas there, most weekends and—believe me—they're not Boy Scouts. The way that place looks, they must spend half their time dynamiting trees. You'd think the law would do something about it. Keeps the old colonel happy, I suppose. That and booze. But what about the squire? Okay—there's the Priory. It's a big estate and he managed it well. But he needed that place more than it needed him. It was the reason for his existence. I remember thinking. *When you give this up, chum, you're finished.*'

'Why give it up?' I asked.

'He wasn't getting any younger. There's no family to

lighten the burden for him. It's common knowledge his wife isn't interested in farming. From what I've heard, he'd been under pressure for months to sell out. Just the land—not the Priory itself. There's a firm over in Brentwell . . . couple of smart operators building a little empire for themselves. All the land they can grab, both sides of the old railway to Furzeby.'

'Wright and Babbacombe?'

He gave me a knowing look. 'Heard of them, have you? Seen any of their land? They've been grubbing up hedges and turning the countryside into a prairie. They farm like there isn't going to be a tomorrow. I don't blame Garland for holding out. His property sticks out like a sore thumb—right in the middle of their empire. But Mrs G was on their side.' He smeared his painted thumbnail across his sleeve. 'Yep. They'll be on Priory land before the year's out. Poor old Garland. Like I said—a man with nothing *interior* to fall back on.'

Ron kicked a stone savagely. It scuttered across the gravel, hit a bollard and splashed into the lock chamber. 'Doesn't make sense. He was determined to hang on—yet he blew his brains out because he couldn't face retirement? Doesn't add up.'

Lampe glanced round as though anxious not to be overheard. 'There's more. He made me promise . . . but I can't see that matters any more. He was facing almost certain blindness. A tumour affecting the optic nerve.' He paused for dramatic effect. 'Not a cheerful prospect, huh?'

Ron scraped his shoe in the dust. 'But people face it every day, without a thought of suicide. Did his wife know?'

'Ah now, that's where we touch on a delicate subject. This dread of blindness—I could see it—know what I mean?—even before he told me. And I couldn't keep it off the canvas. Old Garland didn't like the result. Said I'd made him look like a constipated owl in a thick fog—but that was just talk. What he meant was, I'd said too much in my picture. He refused to have the canvas hung. Put the thing in his cellar, out of sight. But if his wife got a look at it, she'd know what I was saying—even if he hadn't told her himself.'

With great deliberation he added a fleck of paint to his canvas. If he had more to tell, we were not to hear it. Anne was hurrying towards us over the lock gates—her face taut with anxiety.

'Clare's gone!' she gasped.

It took less than a minute to search *Plantagenet*. Pans were simmering on the galley stove. In Clare's tiny cabin the radio was blaring jazz from an American Forces' Network Station.

'I wasn't away more than fifteen minutes,' explained Anne. 'Straight down to the village store and back. When I got here the radio was on, so I thought Clare was in her cabin. I started to fix lunch . . . called her to come and help—and found she'd gone.'

Ron switched off the set and knelt on Clare's bunk to look along the towpath. 'If she's out picking daisies again . . . ' he muttered angrily.

Anne rounded on him. 'She's only a kid. Wouldn't surprise me if she's gone off just to teach us all a lesson. Here she is, miles from home, among strangers . . . involved with an ugly homicide—but when she needs sympathy we read her a lecture on security. Okay she was off-limits yesterday—doing what? *Picking flowers*. When I think what some kids her age could have gotten into . . . Did you *have* to put her down like that?'

Ron fumbled awkwardly with his Rennie packet. 'It was for her own good,' he muttered defensively. 'Anyway, what now? Scour the countryside? Or assume she's striking a blow for juniors' lib and sit tight till she decides to call it off?'

I was making for the gangplank. 'Hope for the best—assume the worst.' I pointed to *Czarina*. 'Think of looking there?'

Anne smacked an open palm against her forehead. 'The most obvious place!'

But Wright's boat was deserted as *Marie Celeste*, yet—like that ill-fated vessel—had a tale to tell. Volumes condensed to an epigram—the reek of cigar smoke, and one more butt in the ashtray.

'I know what you're thinking.' Ron's voice was hard. 'But let's not jump to conclusions. Doesn't have to be his cigar.'

I examined the crushed brown leaf more closely. 'Dare we assume it isn't?'

'Coming back here—after what happened? That's the action of a fool.'

Anne caught my arm. 'Not if he's snatched Clare as hostage!'

Near at hand a diesel engine roared into life. Without waiting for the others, I scrambled ashore and raced along the towpath to the nearest gate. Beyond the hedge a dust-powdered driver was clambering into the cab of his shabby blue tractor. He ignored my shout and as I ran across the stubble I saw his ears were padded in muffs like those used on our basement pistol range in

Whitehall. I reached him as he was putting the tractor in gear.

'Seen a girl around here during the last hour?'

He slipped the muffs round his neck. 'Eh?'

'A girl. Blue shirt and jeans. Has she come this way?'

'Aye. Went up the field with a young feller.' He pointed. 'Reckon that was his car parked yon side the Priory. On the old railway. Come from Furzeby Lane way, seemingly. Been gone—oh, about half an hour since.'

Anne and Ron arrived as he was speaking. Together the three of us hurried towards the disused railway. At the site of the old level crossing, wooden posts had been driven into the hard ground on the Brentwell side and wires were now stretched across the abandoned track. A board had been nailed to one of the posts and on this was tacked a printed notice.

WILDE VALLEY RAILWAY. GRAND OPENING SATURDAY JULY 17—*1976. 3.00 P.M. BRENTWELL STATION. Admission by ticket available at Brentwell Station ONLY.*

Michael Babbacombe, making sure nobody would sneak in by the back door, had unwittingly confirmed what the tractor driver had said. Clare's abductor could only have come from the direction of Furzeby Lane.

Ron slipped out of his jacket and unbuckled the shoulder holster. 'Take this, boyo. I'll nip back to the village, collect the car and meet you where this track hits the road to Furzeby. Be careful.'

The holster struck warm through my shirt as I strapped it on. 'Get the one-inch map from the boat.'

He was already on his way. 'Got a better one in the car. See you!'

Under the blazing midday sun, Anne and I strode along the dusty track. Either side, unkempt hedges—like horse's blinkers—kept our eyes always on the way ahead. All around us whirred hundreds of ladybirds, black against the blue sky.

I fanned a hand before my sweating face to keep the blundering insects at bay. 'We should have checked this way before. I was a fool to assume Wright would make for Brentwell. He could have been holed up anywhere along here since Wednesday night, waiting for an opportunity to deal with us. But why just Clare?'

Anne brushed an arm across her damp forehead. 'Like I said—a hostage. He thinks we've told the police what we saw at the Priory, so he's hoping to buy *out*, using Clare as his ticket. It's happening all the time.'

'Only where the people have some place to go. Wright could ask for a plane to fly him out of the country—but who's going to let him land? He's snatched one kid—not a plane-load.'

'You can bet he's thought about that. He's no fool, David.'

Less than a mile brought us to abandoned Furzeby station. No painstaking restoration here. Six years neglect had produced the appearance of a western ghost town. An engine shed and two platforms linked by a footbridge. Booking hall, waiting room and offices were all on one side of the track.

Jumbled ruts and tyre tracks swung off to the right before reaching the platforms. Beyond, parched grass and tangled undergrowth smothered the old railbed. No vehicle had passed that way in years. Silent . . . isolated —the place seemed to be waiting . . .

We took to the shelter of the hedge and crept

cautiously towards the brick building. From our angle of approach we faced only a blind brick wall. I could read the signs jutting above doorways down the length of the platform. *GENTLEMEN. LADIES. PARCELS. REFRESHMENTS.* If this were Wright's hideout the next hundred yards could prove hazardous.

Only the hum of insects disturbed the oppressive silence. Then—inside that decayed building—a door slammed. Even as my sweaty palm and bandaged fingers slithered on the leather holster, a figure stepped out on to the platform.

Ron Metcalfe.

Stooping slightly he peered in our direction, then beckoned urgently. 'All clear. What kept you?'

We ran towards him. 'You great clown,' I gasped. 'What if he'd been here?'

He shrugged. 'Wasn't, was he? Anyway—I took care. Come on—the car's out on the road.'

We hurried down the station approach—a gently sloping stretch of road already reverting to nature as grass and weeds thrust up through crumbling tarmac. This opened on to the highway beside an iron railway bridge which framed the view towards Furzeby and gave a first glimpse of the airfield where three giant transports writhed and shimmered in the heat haze.

Ron pointed back towards Tongstone. 'Passed the Police House, just round that bend. What say we call there right now? Put them in the picture? Could be we're going to need their help.'

I shook my head. 'You've read our orders. Nothing to compromise the operation.'

He turned away as if in despair. 'Look . . . boyo—face facts! This operation's blown. Our heads are going to roll anyway, so what can we lose?'

But the *deus ex machina* of classical drama was already bearing down upon us in the shape of a powerful Pontiac saloon. Heading for Tongstone it shot under the bridge at more than seventy, the echo of its passage rending the air like a giant's belch. Then came the shriek of brakes as smoking tyres laid twin strips of black rubber on the grey road. A moment later it came whining back towards us and lurched to a halt, dwarfing Ron's shabby Mini like a hen beside its chick.

From behind the wheel emerged a dark-haired man of around thirty dressed in teeshirt and slacks and clearly suffering acute embarrassment.

His apologies began while he was still ten paces off. 'Mrs Meynell, ma'am?' He ran a hand through his hair. 'How do I start saying I'm sorry? You must have been worried sick. Clare Patterson—she's right there in the car. She's okay—she's fine. This whole thing's a mistake.'

Anne regarded him severely. 'You are—?'

'The name's Ferstein, ma'am. Joe Ferstein. Major, US Air Force. You're not going to believe this, but I thought you were holding Miss Patterson against her will. Saw her yesterday while I was fishing down by the river. Recognised her from the pictures in our papers from back home. Guess you won't know this, but she's had 'em all chasing their tails over there. They reckoned kidnapping, for sure.'

Anne took a deep breath. 'So—on the strength of that rumour, you decided to abduct her?'

He winced. 'Ma'am, put that way it sounds bad— but what was I to think? There she was, just the way the papers described her, wandering along the river bank picking flowers. Then along came—well, the gentleman on your right, I guess—and seemed to be dragging her back to your boat. I'll tell you—it didn't look good. So I thought it over, then got down to the river early this morning and sneaked aboard the cruiser. Then I just waited my chance and took it when it came. Seemed like it was my duty.'

Ron choked. '*Duty*? D'you realize what you've done? You've only—' I nudged him into silence.

'Why the change of heart?' I asked coolly. 'I assume you were on your way back to our boat.'

'That's correct, sir. I took Miss Patterson to the base and reported to Colonel Abraham. *Wow*!' His expressive brown eyes rolled at the memory. 'Let's just say he was *not* pleased. It was on the radio this morning that Senator Patterson had issued a statement saying his daughter is visiting with friends here in England. This whole kidnap scare's a mistake.'

'But Clare—didn't she explain she was simply staying with us?' demanded Anne.

Ferstein glanced towards the car. 'Not a word, ma'am. Not one word. If only she'd *said*.'

I caught Anne's eye. 'What *could* she say?'

My wife was not to be appeased. 'She could have stayed right where she was. I don't suppose the major marched her off at gunpoint.'

'*Ma'am!*' protested Ferstein. 'I told her who I was and asked if she'd like to come over to the base. She said yes. That's just the way it was. But when we got talking to Colonel Abrahams, she said she wanted to go back to your boat. When the Colonel was through with me, I felt *so* big.'

The door of his car opened and Clare came slowly

across the road—contrition writ large on her young face. This was neither the time or the place for lengthy recrimination. I tried the more-in-sorrow-than-anger approach.

'This is *not* funny, young woman. I hope you've apologised to Major Ferstein. He could be in a lot of trouble because of you. You *do* realize that?'

She nodded miserably. I turned to the officer. 'If it's any consolation, I'd have done the same, in your shoes. I'll be in touch with your colonel. Try to straighten things out all round.'

He seemed relieved. We parted amicably and Ron drove back to Tongstone while Anne and I returned the way we had come, taking Clare with us. Strange how different the abandoned track seemed now the threat of Wright's presence was removed. As we walked, Clare gave us her version of the noonday adventure.

After Anne had set out for the village store, she had switched the radio to the American Forces' Network in Germany in time for the newsflash of her father's press announcement. It was like an Order of Release for the girl. Suddenly she was free to walk abroad without endangering security or incurring our wrath. It was in those first moments of euphoria that Sir Galahad appeared in the person of Major Ferstein. He could not have heard the news and the temptation for Clare to play damsel in distress was too strong. As for us, well—maybe a joke at our expense would repay the severity with which we had restricted her movements. Without pausing to consider possible repercussions, she followed Ferstein across the fields.

Under the circumstances it was difficult to be angry with the girl. We chided her gently and left it at that.

'Does this mean I can go home?' she asked me.

'I'm not sure. I take my orders from Whitehall, not AFN Munich.'

Anne said, 'There's still this wretched business at the Priory. We'll have to level with the police, and I guess they'll want to see Clare before she leaves.'

I frowned. 'How do we explain all this secrecy? Clare's father has told the world she's simply visiting us. All perfectly innocent. The police are going to ask why we've been keeping wraps on a material witness. In their book that rates as obstruction. They won't like it—and I still can't tell them the whole truth without clearance from the Ministry.'

We reached the old level crossing and turned towards the Priory. Suddenly Anne clapped a hand to her cheek. 'Did I turn off the cooker? That meal's going to be a burnt offering!'

At a trot we crossed the stubbled fields.

'Short cut through the Priory grounds,' I panted.

As we hurried past the old ruins, a window in the Priory flew open. Mrs Frost. 'Quick!' Her voice was shrill. 'The colonel! He's on the rampage. Drunk as a lord and tearing the place apart.'

I stared up at her. 'Where's Mrs Garland?'

'Away in Brentwell at the Registrar's. She can handle the old fool, but he takes no notice of me.'

From within the house came a muffled yell and the sound of furniture being overturned. Mrs Frost put a hand to her head.

'Oh my Gawd, what's he after? I don't want to call the police. Mrs G. would never forgive me. Can you talk some sense into him?'

'I'll be round.'

Even as I spoke the sound of a shot rang through the house to volley its sharp echo against the wall of the old chapel. With the others at my heels I ran round the corner, past the windows of Stephen Garland's study and into the courtyard at the front of the house. Mrs Frost was already at the open door.

'The cellar!' she gasped.

Our footsteps echoed as we followed her across the stone-flagged hall and down a short passage. The cellar door opened on to a flight of stone steps leading down into shadow. By the light of one unshaded bulb I gained the impression of a junkyard cluttered with old furniture.

Keeping close to the wall on my left I descended a few steps. Without a guardrail that uneven stone flight was hazardous. To my right the vaulted cellar stretched away under the house. Andrew Garland was lying down there, his body twisted . . . a revolver near his right hand. I stood very still, my heart pounding from the exertions of the past minute. In the cellar nothing moved. The sight of that gun suggested it might be expedient to summon up the artillery. I pulled the 38 Special from its leather hammock and hurried down the remaining steps.

Silence.

Caught in the chill air a skein of acrid smoke swayed beneath the light. The gun—that familiar Colt Python—had fired the shot we heard. Cautiously I stole across the stone floor to where Garland lay, and, kneeling beside the body, went into the established routine for confirming what I already guessed. He was dead.

Accustomed now to poor light, I gazed round at stacked chairs . . . cabin trunks . . . glass-fronted bookcases—and a fresh-painted portrait. Brendan Lampe's rejected masterpiece. It stood propped against a Victorian rocking-horse—a powerful study of Stephen Garland with the threat of impending darkness closing about him like swirled mist.

Only then did I see what lay beyond the rocking-horse.

Andrew Garland had not died alone. On that cellar floor lay another man, flat on his back—his blazer open like stage curtains revealing a wide bloodstain across the front of his white shirt.

Moving round for a better look I found myself gazing down at a face I knew. Wide-eyed with ultimate astonishment, Colin Wright stared past my shoulder at the cobwebbed lamp on the ceiling.

CHAPTER TWELVE

'Two whole days!' Inspector Young—Brentwell CID—was a very angry man.

Spread on his office desk lay the wasted efforts of Sergeant Pollard and his colleagues—reports on a suicide incident which had suddenly become a murder investigation. The room was crowded with police—uniformed and plain-clothes—and the atmosphere as far as Ron and I were concerned, was decidedly hostile.

The time—three thirty.

Ron fidgetted with a Rennie wrapper. 'Mr Meynell was acting under orders which effectively gagged him.'

'And effectively lost us two days.' The inspector swept a hand across the litter of paper on his desk. 'Pollard's going to love you for this!' A murmur of grim amusement growled round the room. 'You just stood by and watched him make a fool of himself.' Indignant mutters from his staff showed that Young had an appreciative audience. 'Is this what your people call co-operation? Well, you just tell 'em they can take their co-operation and —'

Ron raised his right hand in a gesture of peace. 'My sentiments exactly—but in the meantime, Meynell and I have a job to do.'

'Then I suggest you get on and do it. Just don't expect us to come and hold your hands. From now on we do things by the book. The Chief Constable says you're to be given facilities for an independent investigation into

Stephen Garland's death. Right—you've got 'em, but what you do with them is your own affair. *Independent* means what it says. Now—if you don't mind—we're waiting to start a conference.'

There was general movement in the room. The door opened and the assembled company broke ranks to let us pass. Mass resentment—an unseen force—impelled us forward.

Out in the corridor Ron scowled at the slowly-closing door. 'I take the strongest exception to being treated like some spotty kid caught smoking behind the school bike shed. The Old Man's dropped us in it yet again. *Semper In Excreta*—the Departmental motto.'

'And now?'

'You heard the man. Facilities provided—but we do our own legwork. Let's see what their lab boys have turned up.'

But the pathologist's report on Andrew Garland and Colin Wright was being studied behind the closed door of Inspector Young's office—a circumstance of which we were not informed until we had filled in application forms . . . and waited . . . signed a register . . . and waited . . . answered a barrage of questions. And waited. The ageing plain-clothes coroner's officer who broke the glad tidings seemed to relish his task.

In silence we sped through open country towards Tongstone. Late on that sunny afternoon the road was almost deserted. In nearly ten miles we met only a couple of cars, a tractor and a London-type taxi, looking oddly out of place among meadows and cornfields. I concentrated my thoughts on Colin Wright. When had he returned to the Priory—and why?

The car slowed as we approached the canal bridge at

Tongstone. Over the parapet I glimpsed Brendan Lampe at his easel beside the lock while his wife sat painting a water-can by the cottage door. Bucolic bliss. Beyond the bridge our way was blocked by a herd of cows lumbering ahead of us towards their milking parlour. For half a mile we crawled behind swishing tails, bulging udders and other more basic facts of vaccine existence.

I turned to Ron. 'Your theory about Beth—'

He slapped the wheel impatiently. 'D'you mind? Keep your thoughts to yourself, boyo. Compare notes later if you like, but let me work things out in my own muddled way.'

A lad with a dog shunted the herd into a farmyard on our left and the car squelched forward on to a stretch of unsullied road. We passed the church, *The Haywain*, the store and the dozen houses which made up Tongstone High Street.

'Hey—where are we going?'

Ron stared ahead. 'The Lodge. God—we've been blind!'

He turned left on to the rough track leading to Andrew Garland's home. Fifty yards from the house he slowed the car, swung it broadside across the track and switched off the engine.

'Corking the bottle, boyo. Come on!'

For the second time we stood at the back door of that isolated dwelling.

The bony woman stared at us with red-rimmed eyes. 'Not you two again! Now see here—'

Ron cut her short. 'Alex Howell—is he in?'

'You've no business coming here at this time. The poor Colonel—'

'*Howell*—is he in?'

'No he's not. And what's that to do with you?'

Ron whipped out his ID wallet. 'Defence Ministry—official investigation.'

He brushed past her and headed down the passage to Andrew Garland's study. The place was still a shambles. In a moment he was on his knees, scrabbling among the sheets of typescript which littered the floor.

'Blind!' he muttered. 'I sat here looking at this stuff while Garland was talking—and *then* it didn't register. Ah!' Lifting one page he studied it closely. 'Mmm. Mmm. Here—you're the literary expert. Take a shufti.'

I read.

Western democracy has long championed the cause of political change through evolutionary process—yet exponents of this philosophy have shown themselves ready enough to speed and direct that process by employing the press, and, more recently, other communications media. Ambition, says the Bard, should be made of sterner stuff—an axiom acknowledged by those who would have reformation without tarrying for any. Such men—aye and women too—would set control of armed forces at a premium in statecraft—and if the standing army be not amenable to their doctrines, another force must be raised. When Cromwell lauds his 'plain russet-coated captain that knows what he fights for and loves what he knows' we hear the authentic tones of one politico-military man praising another.

I looked up from the typescript to see Ron watching me. 'Recognise the style, cocky?'

I nodded. 'Stephen Garland—on one of his off days.'

He strode from the room and towards the kitchen. For

a couple of minutes the murmur of distant voices drifted along the passage—then he was back, eyes alight with excitement.

'It's coming together, matey—it's all coming together. Alex Howell's been over at the Priory most days. Doing what? Typing Stephen's mail? That wouldn't take long. He's been typing the latest Garland masterpiece, and for some reason we've yet to discover, he's been feeding a copy to brother Andrew. Look—this is a carbon copy. Tell you another thing worth pondering. Andrew was at the Priory, Wednesday evening—and again this morning, right? Ever stop to ask yourself how he got there? Not on his two flat feet, that's for sure. According to Mrs Thing back there, he could hardly hobble from room to room.'

'Howell drove him?'

'In an old sit-up-and-beg London taxi, would you believe? Andrew couldn't bend enough to get into an ordinary car—so he trundled everywhere in a second-hand taxi, with young Howell up front. I've a few questions for that young feller—but he's gone.'

'We met him on the Brentwell road. There can't be more than one old London taxi around here.'

'Brentwell.' He was toying with the porcelain dragoon's head which lay on the disordered desk. 'Didn't you tell me his sister has been having it off with Colin Wright? This gets more interesting every minute, doesn't it?' He tossed the severed head into the waste basket. 'Let's get after him.'

The extension phone was wrecked but we found a small switchboard across the passage in what must have been Howell's office. From there I called Michael Babbacombe. Wright's death had hit him hard.

'I'm shattered, Mr Meynell. Has the whole world suddenly gone completely mad?'

'It's beginning to look that way, but there's an ugly streak of cold sanity behind what's happened. Have the police told you we're investigating on behalf of the Defence Ministry?'

'No—not a word. Defence Ministry? Where do they come into all this?'

'Stephen Garland worked for us a few years back.'

'I had no idea. But—oh, skip it—this whole business is way beyond me.'

'D'you know a Sandra Howell?'

'Sandy? You mean Colin's secretary? She's not here. Her brother called for her about half an hour ago. She'll be home by now. That's over in Furzeby. Her parents keep the pub there. She's very upset, Mr Meynell. If you're going to talk to her, you ought to know Colin and she were . . . well—'

'I've heard.'

'Have you indeed? Well, it wasn't exactly a dark secret. Rotten way for it to end.'

'Must be making things tough for you, too. Your business—and all your plans for tomorrow . . .'

'Mr Meynell, I don't know whether I'm coming or going. Colin and I weren't all that close, you understand, but I relied on him a lot. Tomorrow's going to be a nightmare. It's too late to cancel arrangements but I certainly shan't be in the mood for celebrations.'

Out on the road we turned left and drove towards Furzeby at a sedate pace. Ron glanced at the speedometer. 'Steady does it. Radar trap along here, this morning when I came through. Crafty devils. Look at this road. Think you were clear of the village, wouldn't you? But you're not. The de-restriction sign's up ahead, round that bend—strategically placed beside the sergeant's gatepost.'

'Booking you would give him great satisfaction.'

'I'll bet. But right now I'm in no mood to gratify the deep yearning of the constabulary.'

We drove past the Police House and a row of cottages just inside Tongstone parish boundary. Another bend . . . the railway bridge—and we were speeding along the open road flanking the airfield runways. Furzeby base was a sprawling self-contained township—a star-spangled manor spread like a carpet of concrete on the English countryside.

In marked contrast the village still seemed to breathe the atmosphere of bygone days. Cottages nestled in flower-decked gardens. Bottle-glass abounded in quaint bow windows. Church, school and pub dominated three sides of the close-mown village green—and in the middle a maypole raised its admonishing finger to heaven.

That maypole troubled me. It cried *Hey-nonny-nonny* in self-conscious tones. I looked again and saw reality behind the idyllic facade. The village school now a prestige residence . . . the ancient churchyard bereft of tomb-stones, now a lawn unembarrassed by intimations of mortality. Georgian bow-windows all from the same factory, cobbled on to plain Victorian cottages.

And the bottle-glass was plastic.

On the billiard-table green, an elegant sign proclaimed *COUNCIL FOR THE PROTECTION OF RURAL ENGLAND—WINNERS OF THE ANNUAL TROPHY FOR THE BEST KEPT VILLAGE . . .*

It should have read *COMMUTERSVILLE UK.*

Round the back of *Ye Olde Crowne Inne* stood a canvas-topped Landrover and the London taxi we sought. A man was emerging from the pub, bent double and dragging a heavy trunk backwards through the narrow doorway.

Ron tapped him on the shoulder. 'A word, young sir!'

Alex Howell spun round and backed against the wall, hands outstretched to ward us off. 'No violence! No violence!' he squeaked.

'Relax sonny. We only want to ask a few questions.'

He cringed. 'You're not the police.'

A girl appeared at the door, her cheesecloth shirt an inadequate transparent bra and the fly-zip on her tight denim jeans straining to keep its teeth clenched. Her hand grasped a leather suitcase. Ron eyed her appreciatively.

'Miss Howell? Special investigators—Ministry of Defence.'

The younger man thrust between them. 'Keep out of this, Sandy. They were at the Lodge this morning, tearing the place apart.'

'Just a few questions,' persisted Ron soothingly.

Emboldened by his sister's presence, Howell spoke truculently. 'We don't have to talk to you.'

The girl regarded him with disdain. 'Shut up, Alex. This was bound to happen sooner or later. Running away isn't going to solve anything.'

Ron's eyes widened. '*Running away?*' He sounded like a reproachful bishop. 'Why so, young sir?'

Howell stared at the ground. 'Start my summer holidays tomorrow, don't I? No need for everything to be mucked up just because of what's happened.'

The girl's eyes said *Believe that if you like.* She beckoned. 'We can't talk out here.'

Pulling the trunk clear of the doorway we followed her into a tiny living-room. She jerked a thumb towards the front of the house. 'Mum and Dad are in the bar getting ready for opening. You two have any sort of identification?'

She studied our cards carefully. 'David Meynell? You phoned yesterday, when I was at Colin's.'

Her brother scowled at us. '*Gestapo*! The Colonel was right. Things he fought against, thirty years ago—they've taken over, right here in England. Brought your rubber truncheons, have you?'

Sandra Howell tossed her head. 'Alex, has anyone ever told you you're a real *drag*? Specially when you get talking like that phoney old fascist.'

'Go ahead—call him all the names you like if it'll make you feel better. He was a real *man*—not like the poncey lot round here with their Martinis and their After Eights. And what about your precious Colin Wright? The perfect gentleman. Left you something to remember him by, *hasn't* he?'

'*Alex!*' The girl's voice cut like a whip.

I laid a hand on her arm. She was trembling—with what emotion I could not tell. 'Colin Wright's death is part of a crazy puzzle,' I said gently. 'Anything you can tell us will be a real help. It must be distressing for you, but—'

'*Distressing?*' Anger squeezed the word in her throat. She shook my hand away. 'I don't know what you've heard, mister defence-man, but if you think Colin's death has broken me up . . . He was a creep. I'm *glad* he's dead!'

CHAPTER THIRTEEN

Heav'n has no rage, like love to hatred turn'd. Nor Hell a fury, like a woman scorn'd.

I envy that poet. With economy—a few deft strokes of his quill—he sketched Sandra Howell. Even the artist Brendan Lampe, for all his painter's perception, could not better that picture.

Her own self-portrait was altogether more flattering—a simple village maiden cruelly wronged. I could applaud her style without believing half of what she said. As counterpoint to her plaintive tale of deception I heard the ambition of a small-town courtesan. That girl knew where she was going.

Her relationship with Wright lasted nearly two years and carried considerable fringe benefits. Within the broad limits of his expense account he was a classic big spender. And—like the Athenians of old—he lived for novelty. A country cottage . . . a sunburst yellow Alfa-Romeo . . . the Wilde River Railway . . . *Czarina*—these were only a few of the objects to which he committed himself and his money during those two years. But each new passion in the ascendancy meant an old love in decline. His Alfa was back in the showroom within three months; his interest in the railway had waned; *Czarina* would have proved a fleeting fancy. Sandra's long survival among his expensive hobbies marked an all-time record. But inevitably the day came when his fickle eye had lighted upon her successor.

'And I was pregnant.' Spoken bitterly, the admission still had the ring of achievement. Her condition was no unplanned misfortune.

Her brother slewed in his chair, turning from her to address an unseen audience. 'So now she has to tell the whole world!'

She glared at the back of his head. 'Offended his little moral scruples, have we? I'm simply giving the folks a clear picture of Colin. Should've thought you'd approve, brother dear.'

He faced her angrily. 'Can't you get it into your stupid head—they're investigating a *murder*? Carry on like this and you'll get them thinking *you* had something to do with Colin's death.'

She laughed. 'That's ridiculous! We know who shot him. Oh—the police aren't saying anything, but the facts speak for themselves. What are you suggesting? That I was going with your precious colonel on the side? *Ugh!*' She turned to Ron. 'I'm not sorry Colin's dead. He *used* people. But for choice I'd have him alive. He wanted me to get rid of *this*.' She patted her midriff. 'No chance! But I'll need time off, and I can't see Wright and Babbacombe holding my job open. So—he owed me compensation . . . and he was going to pay. Oh yes—that's what we were going to discuss, Wednesday night.'

Ron's practised thumb flicked a Rennie into his mouth. 'That was definite?'

'Definite as you could ever be with Colin. He was taking that boat of his down to Tongstone Priory. He might be late back. He might decide to sleep on board. Excuses, excuses. I told him I'd wait at the cottage all night if need be. Huh! Quite like old times.'

'Only he didn't show,' said Ron quietly. 'And he

wasn't at work yesterday. Weren't you even a *little* surprised?'

'I was good and mad. Colin went through life making trouble for other people. Then, when it looked like things were going to blow up in his face, he'd take off. Soon as things quieted down, back he'd come—all smiles. Just like a kid.'

I remembered the man with a gun in Garland's study. 'Was he ever angry . . . violent?'

She threw back her head. 'Hah! Colin wouldn't argue. Sulk, yes; argue—never. He had two remedies for trouble. Charm—oh he could be *so* charming—and money. When you're well heeled, you don't hassle.'

We turned our attention to her brother—a more reluctant witness. He admitted driving Andrew Garland to the Priory on Wednesday evening. Stephen was about to begin his evening meal and his brother had joined him in the dining room. For half an hour Alex Howell had sat in the study, typing from taped dictation. We were mistaken about that typescript. Stephen Garland had been invited to deliver the Carnaby Memorial Lecture, to be recorded for television in September. Alex Howell had been busy preparing the full script of the lecture. At eight o'clock Andrew limped into the study and told Howell to take the car back to the Lodge, then return on foot and meet him in the lane behind the Priory.

Ron interrupted the narrative. 'Thought he couldn't walk more than a few yards.'

Howell sniffed contemptuously. 'Plenty of people ready to write him off as useless. Sure—he was smashed up and he liked—' He tilted an imaginary glass to his lips. '—but he wasn't helpless. Managed a walk, most days. Edge of the wood and back. He had guts.'

'So you met and walked back together through the wood. What time?' I asked.

'Got to the Lodge just after half eight. I remember hearing the Priory clock strike as we came through the wood. Took about ten minutes, going his pace. Must've been around twenty past when I met him. Look, I've been through all this with Sergeant Pollard. Did I hear a shot? Plenty. People potting rabbits all the time. Did I see anything suspicious? How should I know? Met that weirdo from Lock cottage, sniffing round our trees like a bloodhound. Conservation mad. Would you call that suspicious?'

'How about a Landrover?' I asked.

'Landrover?'

'You know.' Ron pointed through the window. 'Thing on four wheels—like that out there.'

'Didn't see one—least, not on that little jaunt. They've got one at the Priory, of course. *Think* it was there when I parked the taxi. Couldn't swear to it, though.'

Asked about the copies of Stephen's typescript he showed embarrassment.

'Not a crime, is it? The Colonel wanted to make sure the facts were right. The lecture's about mercenaries, you know. That's touchy, right now. No sense waiting till it was coming across on television.'

His account of Andrew Garland's last fatal visit told us little. He had driven the taxi to the Priory but stayed behind the wheel as his employer stumbled across the gravel to the front door. Then he had turned the cab and set off for Furzeby.

'Came back here to get some more Scotch. We were running low at the Lodge. The Colonel had been flogging it hard since Wednesday night. I didn't hurry. The Colonel said he might be some time and he'd wait for me. But when I got back, the police wouldn't let me past the gate. I told them who I was and they said to go back to the Lodge and wait for them to come and take a statement.'

'They told you your gaffer was dead?' asked Ron.

'That's about all they *did* tell me. Kept me waiting best part of two hours before they showed up. Had me thinking all sorts of things. Then they said Colin Wright had been shot—and asked if the Colonel was carrying a gun.'

'To which you replied—?'

'I didn't know. All he told me was that he was going to look for a letter. Why take a gun for that? You'll never have me believing he killed Wright.'

Ron regarded him coolly. 'Now that's what I call loyalty. But—human nature's so unpredictable, isn't it? Here you are, your gaffer on ice in the morgue . . . his brother all boxed up ready for a decent burial . . . your sister's boyfriend shot . . . and you—what are *you* doing? Calmly going off on holiday as if nothing's happened. What a remarkable little laddie you are.'

Howell's hands clenched. 'I just don't like being leaned on.'

We drove away as the church clock chimed the half hour after six. Bathed in full glory of the evening sun, Furzeby lay silent and still. Ron shivered.

'No kids,' he muttered. 'Place like this ought to have kids playing on the green before bedtime. Dead, that's what it is. Gives me the willies.' He yawned noisily. 'The long day closes. Not without its moments of interest, wouldn't you say? Heh! *Grand piano.*' He chuckled at the memory. 'What did you make of young master Howell?'

'Cagey.'

'Mmm. Very sensitive about the long arm of the law. That lad's been in trouble. Smell it a mile off.'

'But loyal to his boss.'

'How loyal, I wonder? The way things look, that old sweat has been behind all the unpleasantness at the Priory. Wright may have done the dirty work, but someone a lot closer to Stephen Garland had to set things up. That letter to Beth. All the personal details.'

We were passing the air base. Drawn up before the headquarters building a squad of men stood to attention as the Union colours slowly fluttered down a white flagstaff. Through the open car window I caught thin notes from a distant bugle.

'But I thought you said—'

Ron hunched over the wheel. 'Never mind what I said. I'm not so pigheaded I can't admit to a mistake once in a while.'

'But if Andrew wrote that letter, why was he so anxious to prove it's a fake?'

'What else could he do? You'd told him what you saw at the Priory, Wednesday evening. The suicide theory was blown—and all of a sudden Colin Wright was an embarrassment. If he turned up, all smiles—like Sandra Howell expected—he'd ruin everything. So—young Colin had to be found . . . and stopped. When the gallant colonel went across to the Priory today he may have been hunting for the letter, but he was after bigger game as well.'

We shot under the echoing railway arch and past the

TONGSTONE sign. As the Police House came in sight, I remembered . . .

'Hey—nobody knows about that letter except us. I didn't get around to telling the inspector.'

Ron put his foot on the brake. 'Police van's on the drive. Want me to hold your hand?'

I got out of the car. 'No—you get back to the boat. Anne must be wondering what's happened to us. I'll walk—just as soon as I've made my peace with the law.'

The task was easier than anticipated. Sergeant Pollard proved more tolerant than his superior at Brentwell.

'Come along in, Mr Meynell. How things have changed since we last met!' He led me through his neatly ordered office into a pleasant room furnished in style reflecting good if austere taste. Group photographs of men in tropical uniform adorned hessian-lined walls, together with carved wooden masks and varied examples of African tribal art. The place was comfortably tidy. Books and magazines lay open on tables and chair-arms. Hazy pipe-smoke spread a gentle patina over the whole scene.

He twitched a copy of *Country Life* from one of the club-style armchairs. 'Sit you down. You've saved me a journey—what you might call a diplomatic mission.'

'Look—I'm sorry about what's happened. My orders—'

He waved away my apology. 'Forget it. Our inspector gave you a rough time, eh? Well—you've got to see things from his angle. But that doesn't mean you haven't an angle of your own. I know what your kind of work entails. You're looking at one of the casualties of colonial independence, but in my old job we often had assignments similar to yours. So don't feel you need to apologise to *me*. Put it this way—the inspector's made his point. Now let's get on with the job in hand.'

'He feels that way too—Inspector Young?'

There was a knowing twinkle in his eye. 'He does—only don't expect him to say so. I've been detailed to proffer the olive branch.'

'Then let me give you something in return.' I told him about the letter. He listened attentively then sat staring at the patterned prayer rug by his feet. At last he stood up.

'No use puzzling till we know exactly what's in it,' he said. 'I'll check with CID. They've taken over now.'

I watched him through the open door of the office as he phoned Brentwell. When he returned, his face was troubled. 'They've been over at the Priory this afternoon, questioning Mrs Garland. Not a word about any letter. That woman's beginning to get on my wick. Fair enough—this has all been a big shock to her, but that's no excuse for concealing vital evidence. And I *do* mean vital. I'm afraid I'll have to shut up shop here for a bit, Mr Meynell. CID want that letter.'

Passing through the office he lifted his peaked cap from a peg behind the door. For a moment he looked at me uncertainly. 'Care to join me?'

He was about due for some co-operation. 'Lead on,' I said.

Jamming the cap on his head at a jaunty angle he made for the van.

With the cool of evening came a light wind from the north. Like sheepdogs on the fringe of a straying flock it drove the thick-fleeced smoke of burning stubble across the fields. From the Priory gate the house was lost to sight behind a swirling screen of white. Pungent clouds, like strands of teased lambswool, flooded the van and set us choking. We wound up the windows and slowed to a crawl. Suddenly—dead ahead—the all-embracing greyness darkened and shaped itself into the figure of a man. Head down, handkerchief held to his face, he came stumbling towards us. As Pollard stamped on the brake pedal I felt my body strain against the seatbelt. There was a tearing sound as our tyres locked on the gravel. I found myself staring ahead, fascinated—as though watching action on television. The man's eyes grew round with fear and he thrust out one splayed hand to push death away. He was actually touching the bonnet when we stopped. Then—such is the resilience of humankind—he patted the bonnet, wagged a reproving finger at Pollard, and trudged on into the swirling smoke.

The sergeant restarted the stalled engine and straightened his cap. 'Brendan Lampe. Wanders about here as though he owns the place. According to his philosophy, I suppose he does.'

I waited for further revelations of the painter's ideology but Pollard put the van in gear and drove the rest of the way to the Priory in silence.

The doorbell had been repaired. Its shrill tone deep within the house brought Beth hurrying to greet us. She looked drawn and worried. Her hair was pulled back into a pony-tail and there were shadows around her eyes which owed nothing to make-up. A sombre dress of dark grey accentuated the paleness of her face.

She seemed surprised to see us. 'David! Sergeant Pollard! I thought it must be Brendan Lampe back again. What a *strange* man he is.'

The sergeant looked at her sharply. 'Not been bothering you, has he, Mrs Garland?'

She smiled, 'Heavens, no. He came to express his sympathy—and to ask if he could borrow his portrait of Stephen. Something to do with a copy he wants to make. I know artists are supposed to live on a different plane, but—really! To think he could just walk in and collect the canvas—at a time like this! I told him it wasn't something I could agree to on the spur of the moment—and in any case, the police have said nothing's to be disturbed, down in the cellar. He took some persuading.'

'Did he indeed?' muttered Pollard grimly. 'I'll have a word with that young man. Can't have you being harassed, Mrs Garland.'

'Oh no—please don't bother. He wasn't a nuisance. Just . . . *odd*. Now—come in, both of you. I've an awful feeling you're here to ask more questions.'

We crossed the hall to the parlour. Even in that exquisite room the shadows of tragic mystery seemed to be gathering. Through tall closed windows I saw the ruined chapel walls rise like jutted cliffs from the sea-surge of smoke. One moment the white billows would break over the ruins, hiding them from sight—then the driving wind would veer and the dark mass would swim back into view.

We sat in elegant chairs which could have graced Versailles. Beth looked from Pollard to me.

'So . . . ?' she prompted.

The sergeant cleared his throat. 'It's like this, Mrs Garland. We have reason to believe that a letter was delivered here this morning, purporting to come from your late husband. Now I'm sure you appreciate that we're dealing with a very different case from what we imagined yesterday. The evidence we now have suggests your late husband's death was neither accident nor suicide. On top of that, the unfortunate occurrence here, early this afternoon, is almost certainly linked with what happened Wednesday evening. In view of all this, it's most important that we know what was in that letter.'

'Oh dear.' She was toying with an ivory paper-knife from the Regency writing-desk. 'I was afraid you'd ask that. The fact is, Sergeant, I've destroyed the letter.'

'*Destroyed it?*' Pollard was incredulous. 'But Mrs Garland—'

'I know, I know—it was stupid of me. But I did it this morning before I knew—before any of us knew—that my husband was murdered. Look, Sergeant, you said yourself his death could have been an accident. That was bad enough—but *suicide*! It seemed so terrible . . . such a denial of all Stephen stood for. I just couldn't bear the thought of . . .' Her voice trailed away and her shoulders drooped.

Pollard stared. 'Mrs Garland, this is a very serious matter. Your husband *couldn't* have written that letter. If only we could have seen it, we might have discovered who sent it—almost certainly the person responsible for Mr Garland's death. Now—' he coughed. 'I have to ask you this. Are you being completely open with us? Has that letter really been destroyed? You do understand what I'm saying?'

She nodded dumbly and I could see tears in her eyes. 'I . . . I burned it. If you want to know what was in it, I can tell you—word for word. I know that by heart. It was so . . . so genuine. Who could have done such an evil thing? It must be someone who knew Stephen really well.' She looked at me with pleading eyes. 'I told you what was in it, didn't I, David? His friends . . . the

Department. Who'd know about that?'

Pollard clicked his tongue. 'Well—what can't be cured must be endured, as they say—but I'll have to report this, Mrs Garland. My Inspector's going to be none too pleased, and the coroner may have some hard things to say. Tell you what, though—you sit down tonight and write out what was in that letter. Then at least we'll have *something*. Try and remember anything that maybe struck you as a bit odd. You know—not like your husband's way of putting things.'

'Was it Stephen's handwriting?' I asked.

She rubbed the back of her hand across her eyes—the action of a hurt child. 'But of course. That's why I never dreamed it wasn't genuine.'

The sergeant frowned. 'Mind if I ask the significance of that, Mr Meynell?'

'Something Andrew said, this morning—about Stephen typing all his correspondence.'

He looked across at Beth. 'Was that so, Mrs Garland?'

'I . . . I think he—yes, he did type a lot of his letters. Business ones. But when he wrote to me it was *always* in his own hand.'

Pollard and I left together. A model of sympathetic deference as he said Goodbye to Beth at the door, by the time we reached the van his suppressed fury was at the point of eruption.

'*The stupid bitch!*' he fumed, stabbing the wrong key in the van door in his rage. 'Doesn't she realise the damage she's done?'

He found the right key and, still seething, drove off in a flurry of gravel from protesting tyres. I watched the van career down the drive. By now smoke from the fields had cleared but a sharp smell of burnt straw still hung in the air.

Strolling past the gutted east wing and round a corner I came to the stable yard. Through the open doors of the old coach-house I saw Stephen Garland's dark green Wolseley, Beth's black customised Mini beside it, and a couple of old horse carriages.

No Landrover.

As I climbed wearily aboard *Plantagenet* Ron hailed me from the saloon.

'Come and have a drop of the old *Southern Comfort.* Steadies the nerves.'

I threw myself onto one of the settee berths and reached for the proffered glass. 'Not that they need steadying—but any excuse.'

He chortled with secret merriment. 'They will, boyo—they will. Been on the blower to the blue people at Brentwell. Seems we're all buddy-buddies again. Got the reports on Wright and the Colonel—no trouble at all. Want to hear 'em? Course you do. Pin back your lugs. Andrew Garland? Pickled to the eyeballs. Broken neck after taking a nosedive off those cellar steps. Some time during which brief downward glide—or possibly the moment his old mercenary nut hit the deck—his finger squeezed the trigger and a bullet sped on its way up the spout of his Colt Python.'

I sipped my drink. 'Hard luck on Wright.'

'Not so, matey. You really should have taken a closer look at his young nibs before pounding upstairs to dial nine-nine-nine. That bullet in his ribcage came from a sporting rifle. What's more, he wasn't killed there in the cellar. He was shot somewhere else . . . dragged along all limp and unprotesting like . . . then bumpy bump down the cellar steps. And—just to make your day complete—he's been dead nigh on forty-eight hours.' He raised his glass. 'Cheers!'

CHAPTER FOURTEEN

Dinner that night was the most relaxed meal we had known all week. No gourmet's delight—just honest plebeian fish and chips, provided—courtesy of *Maître* Metcalfe—to gratify the express desire of young Clare. The prospect of quitting England without sampling this gastronomic miracle in its native setting was anathema to her. A mad dash to Brentwell . . . frantic search for a back-street chippie—and four portions of cod-and-tenpennorth were borne to our saloon table with all the ceremony of a traditional boar's head. Wrapped—but of course—in a month-old copy of the *Sun*.

Whenever I recall that meal—and the memory is often with me—I seem to be an observer, standing apart from the group around the table and possessing knowledge which lends poignancy to their animated conversation and the frequent explosions of mirth. I watch the four of us hungrily devour our food and speedily empty the cider flagon Ron had collected from *The Haywain* on his way from Brentwell. I see Anne clear the table for coffee and hear a note of seriousness enter our conversation as we review the latest developments in the Garland case. I watch myself light a cigar and Ron unwrap another Rennie—and all the time I know that those four people will never again sit at a table together as in that moment of remembered time. 'And I can tell you *when* he died' I said.

Anne finished pouring her coffee. 'Colin Wright? I'll buy it.'

'Eight-forty, Wednesday evening. No—I beseech you—no applause. *How does he do it?* you ask. Simple. Cast your minds back to this afternoon. We're standing in the Priory garden, between the house and the old chapel. At that moment, Andrew Garland, gun in hand, is launching himself from the top of the cellar steps. Now—what do we hear?'

'Bang!' Clare stuck out her fingers and flexed her thumb to imitate a revolver.

Anne was frowning. 'No . . . wait a minute. Something else. *Bang . . . smack!* We got the echo from behind us—the chapel wall, I guess. Is that what you mean, David?'

'Exactly. *That's* what I heard on Wednesday night when we were hiding in the old monastery. *Bang . . . smack!* Only I was so sure Wright was firing at me, I convinced myself I'd heard his bullet hitting the wall away to my left. In fact I heard the echo of the shot that killed him, somewhere in the house. And that's been the trouble right down the line—we've put our own interpretation on what we saw. Stuck behind that screen in Garland's study, when Wright was standing in the door, everything seemed so *obvious*. That certainly wasn't the time to march out and say "Pardon me for asking, friend, but *have* you just shot this man? and *are* you in fact about to blow us away because we've interrupted you? Or do my eyes deceive me?" No—I made up my mind in one tenth of a second. Make a decision under that kind of pressure and it sticks. Now if I'm correct about the time Wright was shot, that means somebody else was at the Priory. In which case it's just possible that Wright didn't shoot Stephen Garland after all.'

Ron leaned back and folded his arms. 'But this other

person did. That what you're saying? Now hang on. That would mean. . . Hmm.' He relapsed into silence.

'Mean *what?*' demanded Clare.

He put his face close to hers. 'Go away, you terrible child. I'm *thinking!*'

She grinned. There was no malice in his words.

Anne said, 'Wright didn't *look* a killer . . . he didn't *sound* a killer . . . and Andrew Garland didn't think he could *be* a killer.'

'Huh—the tin soldier!' Ron pushed out his lower lip scornfully. 'Don't set much store by anything *he* said. My money's still on him as the brains behind the operation. They're both at the Priory when you turn up. They hear you arrive. Wright comes in to investigate . . . doesn't spot you in the study but hears you making your getaway through the window. So—back he goes to the colonel. 'Did they see you?' asks Garland. Wright can't be sure—but it's unlikely. Now *that's* the moment he becomes expendable—so Garland brings him down with a sporting rifle borrowed from his brother's gunroom. How's that grab you?'

'It doesn't?' I said bluntly. 'It doesn't square with Alex Howell's evidence. Andrew Garland was in the lane behind the Priory by twenty past eight. *We* didn't get to the house till half past. And what about that Landrover belting away from the scene half an hour later? But keep trying.'

'Hmm. *Howell.*' Ron leaned back and closed his eyes.

Anne glanced at the brass chronometer on the saloon bulkhead. 'Hey! That's never the time! This conference is hereby adjourned. One volunteer for dish-washing step in front.'

Clare thrust a cup and saucer into Ron's hands. He

stood up and glared at us. 'You rotten lot! Who provided that gargantuan repast? Who risked life and limb, hacking a way through the milling mob in *The Haywain* just so you could sit around guzzling applejack? Who—'

She added another cup to his burden. 'Who hasn't done one single chore since he came aboard?'

I left them busy stacking china in the galley and went on deck to check the mooring lines. Time had crept by unnoticed. It was close on midnight and a moon, just past full, was bathing the countryside in bright silver. From the cabin top I could see the Priory across the meadows, every detail crystal-clear like a stereoscopic black-and-white photograph. As candlelight can flatter ravaged features, so the moon restored something of the vanished glory to the fire-gutted shell. Even the old monastic ruins looked less forlorn than in the harsher light of day. Deep shadows created an illusion of walls once more raised to full height. I stood for a while studying the scene, my eyes ranging over house and gardens. Then I looked beyond, towards the abandoned railway . . .

A dark shape was moving slowly across the burnt stubble towards the Priory.

Cupping an ear I turned my head to catch the whine of a car in low gear.

In a moment I was across the gangplank and hurrying along the towpath. Pattering footsteps pulled me up short.

'Where are we going?' demanded Clare.

'You're going back.' I turned and hurried on. She caught up with me by the gate into the meadow.

'*Please.*'

No time to argue. 'Then keep your eyes and ears

open. Someone's visiting the Priory and being mighty secretive about it.'

We crossed the meadow and reached the ruined cloister. 'Easy along here,' I whispered. 'The stones are uneven.'

She tugged my sleeve. 'D'you think it's spooky?'

'No I *don't.*'

'Neither do I. I kind of thought I might.'

'Will you stop talking and *listen?*'

We crept through the roofless infirmary and emerged into the moonlit garden. Before us rose the house, its southern windows ablaze with reflected silver. From the stableyard beyond the gutted east wing came the subdued noise of a car's engine. I halted and Clare, close on my heels, cannoned into me with a muffled squeak.

'From here on we tread very softly,' I whispered. 'This could all be completely innocent—somebody paying a social call on Mrs Garland, though at this time of night I doubt that. On the other hand, it could be dangerous—so do exactly what I tell you. Keep ten paces behind me—and out of sight. If I get into any kind of trouble, don't wait—run back to the boat and fetch Mr Metcalfe. Understand?'

She nodded. Thirty feet apart we tiptoed across the gravel drive. Before we reached the house, the sound of the engine died away. Hugging the wall I passed the projecting east wing and came to the archway leading to the stables. All was silent. Cautiously peering round the corner of the arch I gazed across the cobbles of the shadowy yard. Nothing moved. The coach-house doors stood open but beyond was only a black void. No-one with a lust for life would venture across that moonwashed yard and into the sinister blackness. Motionless I waited while sleep-walking seconds tottered slowly past. From within the coach-house came soft creaks and metallic clicks—unmistakable sounds of a hot engine cooling.

Suddenly a loud whirring reached my ears and immediately the chimes of the stable clock beat down on me—each stroke amplified by echoing walls. Midnight. Instinctively I checked my watch. The luminous dial showed five minutes after twelve—and that watch is accurate to the second. Despite the tension, I smiled. What cared Tongstone for the temporal niceties of Greenwich? I guessed that even conformity to British Summer Time was no more than gracious concession to the needs of visitors like myself. Tongstone—house . . . monastery—was essentially timeless.

The sound of the bell died away and for fully five minutes more I stood waiting by the arch. Then, noiseless in my deck-shoes, I whipped round the corner and crept along in the shadow of the yard wall. A minute later I was in the coach-house. Ranged in order stood the varied equipages which had served the Priory for more than three generations. As my eyes accustomed to the gloom I could see them all. A nineteenth-century gentleman's carriage . . . an Edwardian dogcart . . . Stephen Garland's Wolseley . . . Beth's Mini—and a canvas-topped Landrover.

No surprise—the fading fumes from its diesel engine had confirmed my suspicions before I reached the coach-house. I hurried back to Clare but even as I was telling of my discovery we heard a car at the drive gates. Its headlights flickered between the trees, then vanished as the noise of its engine died. Half a minute later we could see a figure hurrying towards us, keeping on the grass verge as if anxious to avoid making any sound.

I whispered in Clare's ear. 'Everybody wants to get into the act. Keep back in the shadows.'

The hurrying figure came closer and I saw moonlight glinting on the shiny peak of a cap and striking sparks from the metal buttons on the front of a uniform jacket.

We stepped forward. If our sudden appearance startled the constable he gave no sign. 'Who's that?' he demanded, evenly.

'Meynell. Ministry of Defence.'

He came closer. 'Ah—recognise you now. You were over at Brentwell when I came on duty. And this young lady?'

'Clare Patterson. She's a guest aboard our boat, across there on the canal.'

'Ah—the American girl. And may I ask what brings you out here, this time of night?'

'A Landrover,' said Clare.

The peak of his cap shadowed his expression but I could tell he was in no mood for wit.

'She's right,' I explained. 'We saw this Landrover sneaking across the fields and came over to investigate.'

'You must have good eyesight, sir—identifying a Landrover, that far off.'

'I didn't. It was just a dark shape. Had the headlights been on, I probably wouldn't have thought any more about it. But it all seemed so . . . *furtive.* It's in the coach-house right now. Been there about ten minutes. See for yourself.'

He strode across the yard and examined the coach-house thoroughly with the aid of a flashlight, checking car registrations against a list in his notebook.

'You arrived at the right time,' I said.

'How's that, sir?'

'Saved us a walk to the Police House to report this.'

He looked at me oddly. 'Report *what*, sir? This Landrover is registered to the late Stephen Garland. It wasn't being taken and driven away. According to what you've told me, you simply saw it being moved across private land.'

It was the wrong end of the day for explanations. 'Listen,' I said, wearily. 'I've already told Inspector Young we saw a Landrover leave the Priory shortly after Stephen Garland was killed. It could have been this one. It wasn't here this evening when I checked. Now it's turned up, in the middle of the night. That may not constitute a felony, but it's mighty suspicious and I'd like it reported. Incidentally, what brought you along at such an opportune moment?'

'Routine surveillance, sir. A lot's been happening here at the Priory, these past few days—and there's a lady alone in the house, remember. We like to keep an eye on things.'

Perfectly plausible—but he spoke in the bland tones reserved for dealing with the general public. This was polite non-co-operation. He was hiding something.

In *Plantagenet's* saloon the smell of my after-dinner cigar had turned stale. With Clare asleep on the far side of a thin bulkhead the three of us were in conference—*pianissimo*.

'That was no routine patrol,' I said emphatically. 'Car parked down by the gate. Copper sprinting up the drive. He'd been tipped off. Why should he have a note of that Landrover's registration? All that dimbo rubbish about it not being nicked—that was just to make me think they're not interested.'

'Could it have been Beth?' asked Anne. 'The tip-off, I mean. She saw—or heard—you and Clare prowling round the place, and called in the police.'

'Then why didn't they knock on the door and reassure her, once they'd found out who we were?'

Ron leaned back on the settee and stretched his arms. 'I don't get it. When I phoned Brentwell this evening, the blue people were really helpful. Now they're back doing things by the book.' He yawned. 'That Landrover bugs me, boyo. Whoever brought it back to the Priory was taking a colossal risk. Suppose the police had been waiting for him?'

I had a sudden thought. 'No—let's suppose something quite different. *X* equals the unknown, right? The person who shot Wright, set up Stephen Garland's body to look like suicide and then took off in that Landrover. Now if *X* is also the person who brought the Landrover back, one thing's for sure—*X* isn't Andrew Garland. Dead men have limitations. They don't tell tales and they don't drive cars. Now suppose *X* doesn't know about today's—*yesterday's* excitement. He doesn't know Andrew broke his neck in the cellar, so he won't know we've discovered Wright's body. As far as he's concerned, we've been taken in by the fake suicide. That suggests *X* has been away from Tongstone, maybe establishing an alibi. But he has two items of unfinished business to attend to. *One:* Return the Landrover. *Two:* Retrieve Wright's body from the cellar. Tonight he's achieved the first. You're quite right—it *was* risky, unless he had no reason to think the police would be around. Suicide isn't a crime—hasn't been for years. Once the facts of the case were established—and Sergeant Pollard or his constable could do that—there's no reason for the police to be involved—and certainly not the CID. Yes, I reckon *X* has been off the map since Wednesday night and doesn't know what's happened.'

'In which case,' said Anne, 'he still thinks he has to recover Wright's body. Is that what he planned to do tonight—only you disturbed him?' She bit her lip. 'What puzzles me is why he didn't remove the body, Wednesday evening. He had the jeep. Why pass up a chance like that?'

I nodded. 'Only we don't know where he went when he left the Priory that night. Maybe he was working to a tight schedule which didn't allow time to ditch Wright's body. In any case, he'd be a fool to drive around in a vehicle so obviously connected with the Priory.'

'So he was a fool to take it,' said Ron.

Anne stood up. '*Needs must when the devil drives.* I think David's right. He was working to a schedule and we messed it up. That's why he took the jeep. And he couldn't drive around in it, so it's been hidden since Wednesday.'

She stifled a yawn. 'I'm for bed—but I leave you with this thought. He took a big chance, coming back tonight. Now that suggests just one thing to my simple female brain. If it was dangerous to bring the jeep back, it must have been even more dangerous to leave it where he'd hidden it.'

CHAPTER FIFTEEN

Saturday July 17. We slept late. It was nearly nine when my mind thrust its reluctant periscope from the waters of Lethe. I took a swift one-eyed squint along the pillow to Anne's tumbled blonde hair and prepared to submerge again, but persistent knocking on *Plantagenet's* metal hull forced me to surface.

As I sat up, Anne spoke sleepily. 'Brace yourself, world—here he comes!'

I pulled on an all-concealing bathrobe and stuck my head out of the window. On the towpath stood a small woman with a large briefcase and a large man with a small camera.

'Yes?' My voice was husky and my mouth still tasted of cigar.

The woman stopped pounding our hull and bore down on me. Around thirty, she was smartly dressed in orange slacks and white cotton shirt with a brown cord jacket draped across her shoulders. Her companion—a foil to this fashion-plate elegance—wore an ill-fitting blue denim suit in which he appeared to have spent the night. Restlessly.

'Mr Meynell?' She spoke as one whose quest had been long and arduous. 'I'm Margaret Appleby from the *Guardian*. Can we come aboard?'

I rubbed my eyes. 'We've only just woken up. What's this all about?'

'A story . . . photographs. You *do* have Clare Patterson with you?'

I blinked at her.

'Oh, come on, Mr Meynell,' she pleaded. 'That girl is news, right now. You'll know there's been a kidnap scare in the States.'

Behind me, Anne whispered, 'Get rid of her. I'll make sure Clare keeps out of sight.' I heard her scramble out of bed.

I stuck my head further out of the window. 'We don't care what's happening in the States. We don't even care what's happening in England. My wife and I are on holiday. Strange though it may seem, we're actually trying to get away from newspapers . . . television . . . . radio—the whole sensation racket. You're intruding on our privacy. Please go away.'

'Oh come on, Mr Meynell,' she repeated, 'Surely you'll agree the public has a right—'

She was interrupted by a bellow from the stern of the boat. I leaned out to see Ron, clad only in shabby jeans, his thinning hair bushed out from his head like iron filings on a bar magnet. Not a sight for the squeamish.

'Don't you understand English?' he roared. 'The man said *go away*. The audience is ended. Depart. Sling your hook. Fade. Blow. You're engaging in unwarranted harrassment of a private citizen. The Press Council is very touchy about such things. Which paper did you say? The *Guardian*. Right—we'll soon put a stop to this. Thank God for radio telephones.' He disappeared below.

For a moment the woman stared after him, then she began tapping urgently on the saloon window. 'Hey! Let me explain!'

Ron's tousled head reappeared at the stern.

'All right—I'm not with the *Guardian*,' she admitted. 'Not the one you mean. I'm Furzeby correspondent for the *Brentwell Guardian*—and that's in a different league. It comes out once a week and I provide scintillating copy—like who served tea at the Women's Institute and who sent floral tributes to the latest funeral. But I do free-lance work as well—and Vernon here supplies the pictures.'

'Morning,' said Vernon. He made it sound a question.

'I got to hear about Clare Patterson being here with you—and how that Air Force major thought he was rescuing her. I like it. I like it. Human interest and all that. See what this does for me? No one else is on to it. I've got a clear field and a head start. Give me an interview and some pix and I'm made. Phone the story to the States—'

'There *is* no story,' I said quietly.

'Ah!' She wagged a finger. 'I know different.'

I tugged the gaping robe across my chilly chest. 'A word of advice, Margaret Appleby. Stick to Institute teas and funeral flowers. I don't know where you got hold of that nonsense you call a story. You want to make a fool of yourself? Okay go ahead. Call New York, or wherever. The Post Office can do with the money. But involve *me* and you'll be in big trouble. Now—I have things to do.'

I pulled my head in and shut the window. Struggling into my clothes, I hurried to the saloon and met Ron returning from the rout of our besiegers. He shook his head morosely. 'We boobed there, boyo.'

'She's gone?'

'Oh, she's gone—but for how long? No—I'm afraid

our customary *aplomb* deserted us. All we've done is convince her there's a bigger story than she'd realized. If we'd tossed her a crumb of comfort she'd have gone away content. As things are—she'll be back, and I've a nasty feeling she's going to call up reinforcements. She's right, y'know—young Clare *is* news. That girl's been at the centre of a coast-to-coast mystery in the States. Any minute now the media are going to realise she's also at the centre of the Garland mystery over here.'

I glanced through the open door and along the deserted towpath. 'Are you suggesting we prepare to repel boarders?'

He massaged his forehead thoughtfully. 'Either that or clear out. If we stay, we must have a story ready—but what? When I called the Department yesterday they said it was okay to come out into the open, but I couldn't get anyone to tell me how much can be released for public consumption. You don't just take the wraps off an operation like this. See what happens when the Old Man's away? Nobody's prepared to accept responsibility—so we're left holding the baby.'

We discussed the situation over breakfast. Our options were few. Involvement with the Garland case demanded we stay close to the Priory, yet a move to an hotel would only mean exchanging one beleaguered fortress for another. The media would be on to us within an hour—and what would they find? Clare Patterson, daughter of an American senator who was already something of a mystery man, in the company of her English friends who just happen to be Defence Ministry officials investigating the murder of a former agent. The Great British Public might be mildly interested. In the States they would go wild.

Reduced to the proverbial Hobson's choice I set out alone across the meadow to the Priory. Ten-thirty—and another disgustingly glorious day. Overhead, clear blue sky and the blazing sun. Underfoot, dust and parched brittle grass. That morning, a score of cows had been driven into the field and left to forage the scant pasture. Above each patient beast hovered a cloud of flies, but the eager clamour of those insects was drowned by sounds unknown for a decade in that peaceful countryside. From the direction of the old railway line came the amplified thunder of a steam engine at full throttle. The Wilde Valley Railway was in business. What if two of its luminaries had taken a one-way trip to that great terminus in the sky? The show must go on. Over in Brentwell the souvenir tickets were thudding in and out of the veteran date-stamp machine, while down the line loudspeakers were creating the illusion of crack locomotives in steam.

As I came through the monastic ruins and out into the rose garden I could see Beth standing beside a stone sun-dial, deep in conversation with a young man in a light grey suit. She caught sight of me and beckoned. As I approached, her companion turned and I saw he was wearing a clergyman's collar.

'Vicar, I'd like you to meet an old friend—David Meynell from London. He and Stephen worked together at one time. David, this is Mr Undercliffe.'

The young priest seized my hand in a double grasp, jerking my arm up and down like a pump-handle. Two earnest eyes bored into mine as though to plumb the depths of my soul. 'A sad business, Mr Meynell. Stephen Garland was highly respected round here. I can't believe this dreadful thing was the work of anyone local.'

Beth said, 'I've just been explaining the latest developments to Mr Undercliffe. We'd arranged the funeral for Monday, but now the police say the coroner won't release Stephen's body for some days. I don't know how I'm going to get in touch with everybody. It's easy enough with people in the neighbourhood, but a lot of our friends were coming from London . . . Scotland—all over the place.'

The distant shriek of an engine's whistle drifted across the fields. Beth winced. 'Those damned recordings! I'm sorry Vicar—but it really is the limit. You'd think, after what's happened, they'd have the decency to cancel their celebrations—or at least tone them down. Stephen was their chairman. They might show a bit of respect.'

'I'll get on to Michael Babbacombe,' I said. 'May I use your phone, Beth?'

'Sure. I'd speak to him myself, but I'm afraid I'd end up saying something I might regret. The phone's in the study, David—but of course, you know that. I'll be along in a minute.'

Her visitor took the hint. 'I must be on my way, Mrs Garland. We'll leave it that you'll call me as soon as you have word from the coroner . . .'

I left them talking and hurried into the house.

Michael Babbacombe was full of apologies. 'I'm most awfully sorry, Mr Meynell. To be honest I had no idea the sound would reach that far. I'll get someone out right away to disconnect the speakers nearest the Priory. We're only using the recordings to create atmosphere—a warm-up, you might say. Another hour or so and we shan't need them. And—I say—put in a good word for us with Beth, will you? We're not being callous and unfeeling. Just the opposite. I'm sure old Stephen would have wanted us to go ahead—and so would Colin. God—you know, I still can't believe they're both gone. Have the police come up with any ideas?'

I had nothing to tell him, but he seemed anxious to talk and for five minutes his voice babbled in my ear. Through the open window I watched the young vicar taking his leave—double handclasp, earnest gaze and all. For a while after he had gone, Beth stood there by the sundial staring at the roseate glory of that sheltered garden—though I sensed her eyes saw nothing of the beauty around her.

'. . . to Riverside Halt. I'm sure you'll enjoy it.' Unheeded, Babbacombe had been giving a rundown on the day's festivities. I tried to sound as if I had hung upon his every word.

'Great! Hope it's a success, every way. Must go now. I'll give Beth your message.'

Five minutes later I was sipping sherry in the morning room—another elegant salon across the hall from the study—and explaining the purpose of my visit. Beth listened sympathically while I described our brush with the local press and our fears of further intrusion on our privacy. For the first time I was able to tell her something of the mission which brought *Plantagenet* to moor beside the Priory on that fateful Wednesday. As Stephen's widow she knew better than to ask too many questions and when at last I made my request, her response was immediate and generous.

'Of *course* you can stay here, David. I know it's what Stephen would have wished, and believe me, it's no trouble at all. Matter of fact I could do with some company. Mrs Frost offered to stay here at night but I said No. She's needed at home. Her husband's away at sea and she has three children to look after. So I've been all alone. Thursday night wasn't so bad—but last night . . . ! After what happened here in the afternoon, this house was different . . . Maybe *sinister* is too strong a word—but I certainly felt uncomfortable.' She managed a wan smile. 'I don't mind telling you. I came damn near having a fit of the heebie-jeebies. Could have done with you and your crew around.'

'A couple of us *were.* Around, I mean. I suppose the police have told you about our midnight encounter.'

The afterglow of her smile faded. 'I haven't seen the police since Sergeant Pollard was here with you, yesterday evening. What encounter was this, David?'

I told her about the return of the Landrover. She found the incident bewildering. 'I didn't know it was missing.'

'But weren't you in the garage yesterday? Didn't you see the Landrover wasn't there when you got your car out to drive to Brentwell?'

She frowned. 'Yesterday? Oh—when I went over to see the registrar? Yes, come to think of it, you're right. It *wasn't* there. But that doesn't mean it was missing. Don't look so puzzled, David—it's quite simple. That Landrover's for the use of the estate. We leave the keys in. Lots of people drive it, from time to time. John Buckland, our manager . . . the farm hands . . . anybody. And when they've finished with it, they bring it back.'

'At midnight? Driving around without lights?'

The smile was back, twitching the corners of her soft mouth. 'You make it sound so dramatic. Don't forget—farming isn't a nine-to-five job.'

I sat staring at the wineglass in my hand, recalling my

own words. *We've put our own interpretation on what we saw.* Had we jumped to the wrong conclusion about that Landrover? On Wednesday evening, with the dire events at the Priory fresh in our minds, what more natural than that we should connect the speeding vehicle with Stephen Garland's death? Had we in fact seen nothing more sinister than a farm worker hurrying to complete his task in a distant field?

'You could be right,' I admitted. 'Anyway, the police will check it out. They certainly seemed interested. I got the impression that's what brought them here. The constable expected me to believe it was just a routine visit, but I'm not that dim. As you say, it may turn out to have been one of your estate workers, but there's an equal chance the driver of that Landrover was involved with Stephen's death.'

She set down her glass. 'You're serious?'

'Very. We must have scared him off, last night. But if he thinks Colin Wright's body is still in your cellar, he'll be back.'

She looked at me in open amazement. 'David, you're way ahead of me. Who would know about Colin being in our cellar?'

'The man who shot him and put him there, Wednesday evening.' As briefly as I could I explained. It was clear she still believed Wright had been killed only the previous afternoon. When I had finished she was visibly shaken.

'My God! David—I'm frightened. When I think—' She shook her head in disbelief. 'If you hadn't turned up last night . . . he could have got into the house . . . been wandering around the place . . . and I wouldn't have known a thing. I went to bed about half past ten . . . read or a bit . . . then took a couple of sleeping pills—and hat was me out for the count until eight this morning. 'he sooner you get your things moved in, the better I'll ke it. But—if the police know all this, why aren't they roviding some sort of protection? We're completely solated out here. *Anything* could happen.'

I shrugged. 'Who knows? Maybe that's exactly what ley *are doing*. If they're out to nab a suspect, they won't tick a bobby on the doorstep. There could be half a ozen of them watching the house right now.'

She glanced out of the window as though expecting to ee the local constabulary perched in nearby trees.

My watch said eleven fifteen. I finished my sherry. Time I was off, or I won't get to the village before your ne and only shop shuts. We'll have lunch on the boat, len come across this afternoon, if that's convenient.'

She saw me to the front door and watched me set off own the drive. I had gone no more than fifty yards when le trivial incident occurred which was to set in motion a ain of tragic events.

I put my hand to my hip pocket.

The action had become a habit. A quick pat to eassure myself that my wallet was still in place. It asn't. After our rude awakening that morning I had ressed hurriedly, anxious to discuss tactics with Ron. /allet . . . keys . . . loose change still lay where I had ft them on the dressing-table in our stateroom.

Problem. The village storekeeper could hardly be xpected to offer credit terms to a stranger. I turned and etraced my steps, intending to cut across the meadows *Plantagenet*. My way lay past the Priory and through le old ruins. As I passed the open window of the study I eard Beth's voice—harsh, angry, shrill with fear.

'I tell you they *know*!'

Arrested by that brittle tone I stepped on to th flowerbed beneath the window and flattened myse against the wall. The words were innocuous enough, b this was a Beth I had never heard before. I *had* t listen.

'Calm? *Calm*? How d'you expect me to keep caln He said they could be watching the house right now.'

There was a long silence, and I knew she was on th phone. Very carefully I edged towards the window ar peered into the room. She was seated at Stephen's desk her back to me, nodding from time to time as though agree with what was being said.

'Oh *yes!*' Her voice was heavy with sarcasm. 'Yo know everything, don't you? Why in God's name d you bring it back? . . . What if they did? There's nothin to link it with you. Anyone could have parked it the . . . It *wouldn't* have been on your doorstep—but it's c *mine* all right . . . No it wasn't. It was *stupid!* Bright bo Meynell— . . . Oh, you think *that* do you? Well, you' not the first to be taken in by his blue-eyed innocenc D'you think the Ministry employs complete moron . . . I'm not—*will you listen?*—I am *not* gettin hysterical!' Her voice was growing shriller. 'We've got meet . . . I know what we agreed—but things ha changed . . . All right. All right. Yes, I'll listen.' Even that distance I could hear shuddering breaths as sh fought to master her alarm. 'Yes . . . Yes . . . Twel o'clock. Right. *Here?* Wouldn't it be safer—? . . . A right, if you say so . . . Yes, I'll try to find out . . . I'll ri them now . . . And you.'Bye.'

I heard her replace the phone and move in h chair—then the sound of rustling paper as though s ere turning the pages of a book. A few moments later ie was dialling a number.

'Elizabeth Garland here. Tongstone Priory. Who is iat? . . . Ah, good morning Sergeant. Perhaps you can elp me . . .' She laughed lightly—the sound as false as lastic jade. 'Yes, I'm sure you will. Thank you. It's iis—I understand there were some oddgoings-on ound here, last night . . . But surely you know? Your en were here . . . No—it was Mr David Meynell as a atter of fact and, frankly, Sergeant, what he said is disturbed me. I was wondering—are your people eeping an eye on things, here? We're very isolated, you iow, and I'm alone in the house . . . Ah, I see. Just utine patrols. You think that's sufficient, do you? . . . o, I'm perfectly satisfied. I simply wanted to know . . . 'ell, that's very kind of you . . . Uhuh . . . Yes. oodbye.'

The phone went down . . . swift footsteps crossed the irquet floor . . . the study door slammed shut—and I as away across the drive and sprinting for the shelter of e ruins.

CHAPTER SIXTEEN

For fourteen years I had known and respected Bet Garland. Before her marriage there had been a brie false dawn of mutual attraction which had not survive Stephen's advent. A youthful memory, it had left i mark on our subsequent friendship—slightly exa gerated gallantry on my part; demure coquetry on her We did but jest—as all who knew us realized.

Bright-boy Meynell. No humour had softened th bitter tone in which she spoke those words. Standing b that open window I had experienced swift and savag betrayal which mocked the years of my sincerely offere friendship.

Back aboard *Plantagenet* my breathless report se Ron pacing the saloon carpet.

'I *knew* it!' he muttered, smacking a fist into h cupped palm. 'She *had* to be involved. But . . . *wh else?'*

Anne stood beside me as I sat hunched on the sette her hand resting gently on my shoulder. 'Darling, I'm s sorry. I'm like Ron—I've had my suspicions of Beth ev since that letter arrived. It was too convenient—t clever.'

I placed my hand on hers. 'Why didn't you say. Y know how much I value your opinion.'

'I wanted to. I rehearsed it over and over in my min but it always sounded mean—like I was saying it out spite. I've never liked Beth. I've tried, but it's no us h, I know I've never had cause to be jealous. You were iends—period. But you were sincere while she always emed to be laughing at you.'

'Always?'

'Uhuh.'

Ron stopped his pacing and looked at the chronom- er on the bulkhead. 'We're wasting time. It's nearly venty to twelve. You're sure you heard right, boyo?'

I nodded. 'They've arranged to meet at the Priory at idday.'

'Then we must be there—but we've got to be careful. just you and I go charging across, they'll suspect ouble. Here's what we do. I'll nip down to the village nd call the police. The rest of you get some suitcases gether and look like you're shifting your gear across to e Priory. Take your time. You want to get there about ve to. That way she won't be able to warn off whoever it she's expecting. From then on we play it by ear. I'll get e car and join you just as soon as I've contacted the ue people.' He hurried to his cabin.

'It's risky.' I raised my voice above the clatter of awers being dragged open and slammed shut. 'We're against a killer with two hits to his credit already. I on't think we've any right to involve Anne and Clare.'

He reappeared in the cabin doorway, hastily strapping the shoulder holster, 'Have no fear.' His hand patted e revolver. 'They've too much at stake to risk more olence at this stage—specially when they see we've vided our forces. God—look at the time! I'm off. See ou!'

A moment later he was gone. We felt *Plantagenet* rock ightly as he jumped ashore.

'Right,' said Anne briskly. 'Let's move. Everybody

grab a case. Shove a few things in—just for appearance: But *hurry!*'

We dragged suitcases and holdalls from their restin places in wardrobes and under bunks, hurling i sweaters, books—anything to hand.

'This is crazy,' gasped Clare, zipping my leather fligh bag. 'We're on collision course with an armed hood an you don't carry a gun. Back home—'

'Shoo!' Anne propelled her through the door. 'Bac home, David got to you just one jump ahead of som very nasty people—and he didn't have a gun the Hardware isn't always the answer.'

Out on the towpath I checked my watch. Ten t twelve. We set off at a leisurely pace across the meadov By now Ron would be in the village phone-box, callin the police.

Sounds of distant music drifted towards us, born faintly from the direction of the old railway. Babb combe and his friends were building up to the gran opening ceremony, scheduled for noon. Even in ou own tense situation I could spare a thought for th hapless treasurer of the Wilde Valley Railway, stru gling with his problems. He was right, of cours Stephen Garland would certainly have wished the day festivities to go ahead.

We were less than halfway across the meadow when saw the jeep. It came bumping and swaying round th corner of the ruined chapel, turned towards the Prio then swerved suddenly and headed in our direction. I top was open and I could see a man in a bright yellow shi behind the left-hand steering wheel, with a woman b side him—long black hair blowing across her face. Th driver raised one hand from the wheel and waved.

'It's Joe Ferstein!' Clare set down her cases and waved ack.

I glanced at my watch again. Seven minutes to. Be-eath shady trees, cattle raised their heads as the jeep oared across the grass and pulled up beside us.

'Hi!' Ferstein's eyebrows lifted at the sight of our urdens. 'Vacation over already? We were on our way o see you.' He turned to the woman at his side. 'My wife ue.'

She brushed the hair from her eyes. 'Hi! Joe feels so ad about what happened yesterday, we just *had* to ome over and—well . . .' She grinned and spread her ands eloquently. '—try to straighten things out.'

Anne smiled. 'No need. Mistakes happen. But—hanks all the same. Look, we can't stop right now. Ve're due at the Priory before twelve.'

'No problem.' Ferstein pointed to our cases. 'Stow hose in the back and climb up beside them. Have you here in under two minutes.'

To refuse would be churlish—and hard to explain vithout further loss of precious time. We clambered board with our luggage and the jeep leaped forward, hrowing up clouds of dust as it swung in a tight circle to ace back the way it had come. We rounded the south-est corner of the old ruins at close on fifty, clinging to he sides of the swaying vehicle as its body leaned over at seemingly impossible angle. Flashing past the chapel e shot down the gentle slope to the sunken lane, turned ight and bounced along the deep ruts to where they wung away towards the stableyard. High walls threw ack the roar of our engine and the squeal of tyres as we hot past the coach-house, through the stone arch and ut on to the gravel drive. With a sound like tearing calico we skidded to a halt beside the front door. Fe stein had kept his word. We had managed the journey less than two minutes. It was exactly three minut before twelve.

He switched off the engine. 'End of the line. Say, M Meynell—we'd hoped you might join us this afterno —or maybe let Clare here come along for a few hour They're opening this private railroad over in Brentwel There's an old-time fair and a vintage automobile ral as part of the show. We'd planned to look in on th celebrations, then picnic some place quiet.'

Before I could consider his proffered peace-pipe, th Priory door flew open and Beth appeared on th threshold, her look of amazement showing she had n expected our arrival. For a moment she stared, ope mouthed . . . then the familiar smile was back. Fam iliar—yet to my newly enlightened eyes an actor mask.

'David! Anne! I wasn't expecting you so soon.' Sh glanced past us down the drive. 'Come along in. An who are your friends?'

I introduced the Fersteins but she was preoccupie her eyes straying towards that distant gateway. Liftin our cases from the jeep, Ferstein and I carried them in the house. He was anxious to press his invitation.

'I can see you're busy right now, Mr Meynell, but we gladly stick around if there's a chance you'll be free late Or maybe Clare . . .'

It was a thought. No need to involve the girl further this affair. I turned to see her following Anne and Be into the hall. 'Clare! Major Ferstein—'

He lifted a protesting hand. 'Make it just *Joe*, huh?'

'Joe's invited you over to Brentwell for the opening

ne railway. How about it?' I looked into her eyes, odding encouragement as I spoke.

'Is it okay by you?' she asked uncertainly.

Anne patted her arm. 'It's a great idea. Thank you, oe. Just one thing—promise you'll keep her away from ny pressmen. They're after a story, but I'm sure the enator would rather she didn't give any interviews.'

Ferstein saluted smartly. 'Understood, ma'am. So appens we have the same problem. One of our boys pened his big mouth in the local pub last night—about esterday's fiasco. I've already had one call from the ress this morning. That's partly why we decided to lend with the scenery for a while. Is it okay if we take 'lare right now?'

Anne's glance passed the question to me. 'Sure,' I aid. 'You ready, Clare?'

The girl turned to Beth. 'May I use your bathroom, Irs Garland?'

'The *bathroom?*' Beth sounded surprised. 'Why, of ourse. It's up—but I'd better show you.' As they moved vay I heard her murmur. 'We do have a cloakroom ownstairs, if—'

'That'll be fine.'

They disappeared beneath an arch which opened un-er the stairs—the passage leading past the cellar to the un-room, the kitchen and the back door.

Through the open front door I saw Ron's familiar Iini coming up the drive. As it neared the house I oticed a man sitting beside him. They both got out of e car together and walked towards us. His companion -Brendan Lampe.

'Here we are, boyo. Just been playing Good Samari-n to our artist friend here. Asked me for a lift as I was setting out from the village. Seems his bike has a flat tyr and he was anxious to get to the Priory.'

Lampe nodded. 'Made a bit of a fool of myself, yesterday. Came marching in here demanding that portrait o the squire. God knows what Mrs G must have thought Felt I ought to drop by and apologize.'

Ferstein nodded a greeting. 'Hi, Brendan.'

'Aha!' exclaimed Ron dramatically. 'Sir Galahad, n less! That your jeep out front?'

Before Ferstein could reply, Beth came hurrying across the hall to join us, the false smile firmly in place.

'And still they come!' she said lightly. 'What is this— convention?'

Lampe stepped forward. 'Mrs Garland—I felt I had t come and see you . . .'

Ron led me away towards the back of the hall. 'Wa Ferstein here?' he whispered.

'No. Met him out in the fields. He brought us in hi jeep. What's all this about Lampe?'

'Dunno, matey. He was in a rare old sweat when picked him up, but I can't think *X* the Unknown woul cadge a lift to his secret meeting. Or is he being clever Maybe—' He stopped suddenly and cocked his head t listen.

'What's up?'

'Shush! Thought I heard something. Yes—back doo Someone's just come in. Hang about while I take a quic shufti.'

I caught his sleeve. 'Could be anybody. Don't mes things up now. If Beth sees you—' But he was gone moving swiftly and silently away down that passage beneath the staircase. In a moment he was out of sight. stood still, fearful lest any movement would attra

Beth's attention. Across the hall, Brendan Lampe was llustrating a point in his earnest conversation with ramatic gestures.

''ullo! 'ullo! 'ullo! What's all this, then?' Ron—fooling round.

The explosion of a gun fired in a confined space roared own that passage and out into the echoing hall. Fool-ardy, I leaped for the archway and rushed forward—to e knocked sideways by the sudden opening of a door in he panelled wall on my right. I hit the opposite wall, lost ny balance with the impetus of my rush, and lay dazed . . winded—looking up at Clare framed in the cloak-oom doorway. Then I was scrambling to my feet and tumbling on.

Back door open . . . haze of gunsmoke in the air . . . Ron huddled face-down near the end of the passage.

I knelt and turned him over gently. His eyes were pen and he was frowning as if desperately trying to emember something. He had taken the shot in his hest, just above the heart.

In the darkness of that passage somebody brushed ast and dashed through the open door. Ron was trying o speak.

'David?'

'Easy, old lad. Soon get you fixed up.'

He smiled and closed his eyes. Then his head lolled gainst my arm.

CHAPTER SEVENTEEN

Anne was kneeling beside me. 'How is he?'

I stared at her stupidly. 'He's dead. I . . . I thought h was talking to someone he knew. Then—'

She gently lifted Ron's limp form from my arms an laid his body on the floor of the passage. Then, without word, she unbuttoned his jacket, pulled the revolve from its holster and pushed it into my hand. It felt warn and the butt was sticky. As I took it we heard an engin revving, out in the stable yard.

She gripped my arm. 'Beth's out there. She's with— whoever did this. Get after them.'

Clutching the gun I stumbled along the passage. Clar was staring at the scene by the back door—Ferstein an Lampe beside her. I grabbed the major's arm an dragged him towards the front door.

'Your jeep!'

'You got it!' As we burst into the sunlight he wa shouting to his wife. 'Out, Sue—*out*!'

Seconds later the jeep ripped furrows in the gravel a we shot forward and slewed round towards the stable yard arch. Away down the drive I could see Sergean Pollard's blue van speeding towards the house. Useles for a cross-country chase. We were on our own—an that was how I wanted it. Ron's death had unleashed dee rage inside me. Prosecuting counsel . . . judge—I ha been both, in a matter of seconds. Now I was determine to be executioner.

I snatched a second to check the gun as we thundered onto the cobbles. Yard deserted—Landrover gone.

Into the paddock—ahead of us a blur of green and brown in a cloud of dust.

Ferstein shouting—his voice jerky with the savage bouncing of the jeep, 'He won't take much catching—but what then?'

'We finish them.' As I thudded up and down on the seat my words fell out like sobs.

We skidded into the lane, crashed into low gear and tore along the punishing ruts.

'They're armed?' bellowed Ferstein.

'Yes.'

He jerked his head towards my revolver. 'Any good with that?'

'I hope so.'

He wrenched the wheel. 'But not like this. Too rough. Same for him, though. We're safe while he's moving. If he stops—watch out!'

Through the dust I glimpsed the Landrover turn right into the field of burnt stubble beside the old railway. Ten seconds later we took the same gateway broadside, broke out of the skid and bounded forward, steadily closing the gap between us and our quarry. Remembering the wire fence which now barred the track to Brentwell I expected the other driver to turn right at the level crossing but the Landrover rocketed through the opening and on to the bed of the old track, ploughing straight into the flimsy barrier of wood and wire. Next moment it was out of sight behind the hedge, but a racing billow of dust showed its speed had not slackened.

'Where the hell's he going?' yelled Ferstein. 'He's headed slap into the railroad show.'

Round a gentle curve—and there, half a mile ahead, Riverside Halt. Crowded. Fairground booths blocking the track. Red, white and blue bunting stretched high over the line. The Landrover slid to a halt.

Immediately, Fernstein slammed on our brakes. 'Down!'

Crouching, I peered along the jeep's bonnet and watched Beth jump from the other car and throw herself at a barred gate. Seconds later it was open, the Landrover was through and she was swinging the barrier shut. Then she scrambled back into the cab.

'She didn't fasten it!' I yelled.

Ferstein let in the clutch and set the jeep at the gate. We burst it open at twenty miles an hour—then up through the gears and away across stubble only recently shorn by the combines. We had lost ground. The Landrover was well ahead and already speeding through a gap in the far hedge.

How many fields did we cross? Three? Four? I lost count. Ferstein wrenched the wheel right and left, weaving a serpentine track among the straw bales which littered the ground. Some, box-like blocks; others, gigantic rolls of tight-packed straw bound with thick twine—Swiss rolls from a gargantuan bakery, each four feet wide by six feet long, set down casually on a ten-acre cake dish. And at each hedge we had drawn seconds closer to the other contestants in that deadly race.

Then, atop the rise in the middle of one vast field, I knew the other driver had blundered. Across his path stretched a narrow strip of woodland bounded by a wire fence with neither gap nor gate in sight. As the Landrover slewed left and tore along the line of that fence, Beth turned towards us, her face pale against the dark background. Suddenly the canvas-topped vehicle stopped and on the instant our jeep shuddered to a standstill.

'This is it,' breathed Ferstein, ducking low behind the wheel. 'Right now our friend down there is deciding whether to turn back and risk whatever firepower we're packing, or stand his ground and dare us to come on.' He sat up, leaning forward and shading his eyes against the sun. 'Wrong again, Joe boy. They're away! Here we go again!'

'Hold it!' I said urgently. 'Can you see them?'

'Not now. They're both through that fence. I caught a sight of the woman's dress and there's somebody else ahead of her, but under those trees it's too dark to see who.'

But I already knew the identity of that shadowy figure. A wild thought had flashed into my mind as I stood in the hall at the Priory, watching Brendan Lampe's dramatic gestures as he spoke to Beth. In our headlong dash across country that thought had blossomed into theory —and theory had been matched by evidence.

'What d'you reckon?' I asked. 'Are they still running, or have they dug in?'

'Running, I guess. That's what this crazy joyride's all about isn't it. They dare not stop now. We'll hit that wood along to the right. See—it thins out there. If we go straight through we could be waiting for them when they break cover on the far side.'

Once again the jeep leaped forward and careered down the hill, bearing to the right and reaching the fence a hundred yards from the Landrover. Ferstein switched off the engine and immedately we caught the sound of band music from the direction of the railway. Over there, real life was still going on.

'A word from your sponsor,' he muttered. 'Once through that fence, keep low—keep moving.'

We scrambled between strands of thick wire and on through tangled undergrowth which grew among the trees. The place was alive with insects—flies, mosquitoes, all homed in on our sweat-streaked faces. Ferstein grabbed my arm and pulled me to the ground. 'Listen!' he hissed.

From somewhere ahead and to our left came unmistakeable sounds of human bodies forcing a determined way between the close-packed trees. Then we were on our feet again and stumbling in pursuit.

It took us five minutes to get through that narrow strip of woodland and when we emerged on the far side we found ourselves in an empty fresh-reaped field. Twenty yards to our left a tall hedge separated us from the point where the others must have broken cover. We raced diagonally across the stubble, dodging between more rolled straw-bales as we made for an open gate—every pounding step costing precious time.

At the gateway we stopped—confused by the sight before us. The combine was in, with a mechanical baler in hot pursuit—two yellow monsters crawling along opposite sides of a rectangle of standing corn. Gargantua's bakery. Huge straw rolls littered the ground. As the rectangle dwindled, hunters closed in—men with shotguns . . . kids with catapults. Deaf to the siren-song of loud speakers on the railway, they had gathered for the customary perquisites of the harvest field.

And the rabbits were obliging. Even as we watched, a tiny creature bounded from cover, took a blast of pellets behind its terror-flattened ears and bowled over, kicking feebly.

Some thirty people were strung out around the stalky slab of chest-high goldripe grain. Were our fugitives among them?

Ferstein's glare-narrowed eyes took in the scene. 'We'll flush 'em out,' he gasped with the confidence of a man accustomed to authority. 'They'll be jumpy as hell, so start running—and make like you know where they are.' He looked dubiously at the gun in my right hand. 'I sure hope you know how to use that thing.'

Then he was off across the stubble, shouting at the top of his voice—right arm thrust forward like a cavalryman leading a charge. It was crazy . . . foolhardy . . . magnificent—and it worked. People turned to stare . . . some pointed with obvious amusement . . . but above the swaying ears of corn I saw one figure stretch both arms together, like a diver ready to take the plunge. And at the extremity of those out-thrust arms the hands clasped a revolver. I watched it sway from side to side, trying to follow Ferstein's erratic movements as he zigzagged across the field. There was a sharp retort and Ferstein dropped like a shot rabbit, rolling over and over across the stubble.

Suddenly people were shouting and running in all directions. Panic communicated itself to the ear-muffed drivers on combine and baler. Both machines stopped—the noise of their diesel engines puttering in silence.

I brought up my own gun in the officially approved manner—feet apart, body forward, arms straight ahead, left hand clasping right, making the Smith and Wesson a metal forefinger thrust towards that distant target. At that range accuracy was impossible—for me—but I squeezed off two shots in obedience to the Rommel dictum: always return fire with maximum speed and power. Make your opponent keep his head down. It worked like a charm. All round the field men crouched and knelt, some even throwing themselves prostrate. No pontiff with arms outstretched to bless could have achieved so reverential a response in so short a time.

But the whole situation stood balanced on a razor's edge. That brief exchange of fire had caught those stolid countryfolk unprepared. Now they were recovering from the initial shock and sizing up the position.

I saw Ferstein—unhurt—crawl for cover behind one of the straw bales. He turned and waved. 'For God's sake tell these folk we're the good guys!' he shouted hoarsely. 'We don't want twenty shotguns pointed our way.'

But before I could take this advice the problem resolved itself dramatically. A few yards to my right a young lad straightened up and began to wave his arms.

'Daft ninnies, the lot o' you!' he shouted at his companions. 'They're having you on. It's Candid Camera!'

A moment later he spun round, doubled with pain and clutching his right arm as the sound of another shot cracked across the field. Marksman shooting—it won a bitter trophy. The startled bystanders, uncertain which of us were in the wrong, doubted no longer. Bending low, a man rushed across to the lad.

'Easy does it, young 'un,' he muttered gently. His words—the way he stooped over the wounded boy—reminded me of those last moments at the Priory with Ron. Black fury surged into my brain.

The man looked my way. 'They're in amongst the corn,' he said.

Crouching, I ran forward and joined Ferstein behind the bale.

'Can we roll this thing?' I demanded.

'Guess so. What's the idea? Cover?'

Together we pushed the drumlike bale forward, kneeling behind it and thrusting it away with hands and shoulders. Yard by yard it rolled closer to the standing corn.

'I hope—' panted Ferstein, 'I hope you realize . . . they can . . . they can hit us on the flank if . . . if we move in much closer.'

'We're near enough.' I handed him the gun, then, scrabbling at the tight-baled straw I tugged loose a handful, fumbled a lighter from my pocket and snapped flame to the bundled stalks. 'Cover me!'

Bent double I sprinted the last few yards to the standing crop. A moment later the blaze had begun. I dragged the flaming torch along the edge until there was a searing wedge of fire, thirty feet wide, surging into the golden heart of that uncut rectangle. Then the torch burned my hand and I tossed the blazing cluster of stalks to the ground.

Ferstein was beside me. 'For God's sake, man—what's gotten into you?'

'The gun—give me the gun!' He seemed about to protest but I snatched the revolver from his hand—then I was running . . . stooping . . . swerving . . . stooping—running again, away to the left down the length of the standing crop, round the sharp angle at its corner and then on again, up the field towards the railway.

At the next angle I straightened up for a swift look back. The fire had taken fierce hold and was sweeping towards me, fanned by a wind from the north. I could hear the angry cackle of flames, but all sight of the blaze itself was now blotted out by thick clouds of smoke.

Suddenly a figure burst from the choking pall, stumbling blindly. Beth—clothes ablaze, hands beating wildly at the flames. Grey clouds swept over her and she was lost to sight. In a brief moment of complete detachment I realized I felt no pity for her anguish.

Then—just as the smoke reached me—I saw a dark shape break from the corn and race towards the railway line. Above the deep roar of the flames, loudspeakers were belting out more brass band music—*Casey Jones*. And Babbacombe had set another of his steam engine discs on the turntable. The thudding of pistons echoed the pounding of my heart. For a moment the fleeing figure was visible—then smoke rolled between us. Gasping . . . choking, I flung myself forward, running parallel with my quarry. A fence loomed in the whirling grey and as I scrambled through I saw the track ten feet ahead. A moment later I was on the chipped stone ballast and peering west along the line for one glimpse of that dark shape.

The smoke cleared and I could see forty . . . fifty feet. The track stretched before me and my adversary stood revealed. With a surge of dread recognition I knew my nightmare had become reality. Shadows on Main Street . . . billowed dust from the desert . . . the final shootout before the credits. And this time there would be no awaking. Even as I watched, his arms thrust forward in that familiar menacing gesture. Flame spurted for one instant from between his clasped hands—and a hammer-blow crashed on to my right shoulder. Knocked off balance, I fought to keep my feet. In that instant I knew my chance hung by a thread. Numbness was yielding to pain. The night of oblivion was falling.

Suppliant hands together, I forced the gun up level with my eyes and took careful aim. A roaring in my ears . . . strident music . . . the gasping old-time locomotive . . .

My finger tightened on the trigger, then turned to putty as impotence thwarted lust and the gun began to droop . . .

. . . and a huge shape materialised in the smoke behind that distant figure, crushing him as a child swats a fly. With one exultant shriek, the first locomotive on the Wilde Valley line smashed him on to the rails and mangled all life from his body.

Consciousness draining, I dropped among trackside weeds as the inaugural train rolled triumphant on its way.

CHAPTER EIGHTEEN

They took out the bullet at Brentwell infirmary. Anne was by my bed to welcome me back from anaesthetic nirvana. One question had tantalized my unconscious—projecting the image of a familiar face to the retina of my imagination. When I opened my eyes, the picture lingered.

'Ron?' My dry mouth made the name into a hoarse croak, but Anne understood. She shook her head. Hope was a dream, but reality a remembered nightmare.

I nodded dumbly. Loss of blood and the effects of the operation had left me with only a child's control over emotion. I closed my eyes again. 'And Beth?'

I heard Anne's sharp intake of breath. 'She'll survive—but she won't be a pretty lady any more.' Her grip tightened. 'I'm sorry it had to be her.'

'She got what she deserved,' I said bitterly.

'I'm thinking about *you*.' Her hand touched my cheek lightly.

'Thick!' I shook my head, bringing a surge of nausea to my throat. 'That's what I am—*thick*! All these years I've thought she and Stephen were really happy together. She's as guilty of murder as if she'd pulled the trigger. Involved up to her neck. That phoney letter—Ron guessed she was behind it.'

Ron. I tried to clear the tightness in my throat. My mouth was rough and dry. 'Can you give me some water?'

She leaned over to the bedside cabinet, poured a glass and held it to my lips. As she moved I caught the whisper of her perfume and its remembered fragrance set a protective screen about us. 'Better?'

I swallowed. 'Great.'

'Good—so now perhaps you'll tell me who shot you *this* time.' She was smiling and I knew this was her way of guiding me from indulgent misery. 'It's the sort of thing a wife likes to know.'

'They haven't told you?'

'Not a word. Joe Ferstein couldn't recognise what was left on the railroad. The police know—I'm sure of that—but they aren't saying.'

'I'll bet! It was that pillar of rectitude and keeper of the Queen's peace—Sergeant Pollard.'

She whistled softly. 'But I thought—'

'Welcome to the club. He had us all fooled. When Beth said she'd destroyed that letter he put on the performance of a lifetime.'

'But you guessed. When?'

'Five minutes too late. When Ron went to investigate who was sneaking in at the back door of the Priory, I heard him say "*'ullo! 'ullo! 'ullo? What's all this then?*" Then—well, you know what happened, and it happened so fast there wasn't time to think. But later, rattling around in Joe Ferstein's jeep, I got to asking myself why Ron went into his bobby-on-the-beat routine. Obviously he was talking to someone he knew . . .. someone he didn't suspect—but there was something more. Ron's sense of humour is always spot-on. So if he says "*'ullo! 'ullo! 'ullo!*" it's funny. Not because he puts on an accent but because it's *appropriate*. Am I making any sense?'

She nodded. 'You mean a comedy cop routine is

appropriate if you're talking to a cop. Well—you won't get me saying "Who loves ya, baby" to any of the officers I know back home—but . . . Ron? I guess you could be right. He was like that.'

'I couldn't get the idea out of my mind. But Ron only knew a couple of officers on the local force—Inspector Young and Sergeant Pollard. I couldn't imagine him talking that way to Young. But—*Pollard?* I'd just seen his van coming up the drive, so that ruled him out. Or did it? This whole wretched affair has been loused up because we've seen things—and put the wrong interpretation on them. We saw Wright with a gun in his hand, and convinced ourselves he'd just shot Stephen. I heard a shot and made sure it was meant for me. Wright's body in the cellar—I was certain he'd just been killed by Andrew Garland. Now somewhere along the line I had to start learning from my mistakes, so I thought *That was Pollard's van, but he didn't have to be in it.* Then things started clicking into place. He had everything going for him. Investigating officer . . . first on the scene . . . reporting what he *wanted* reported, the way he wanted it to look. Remember what we said last night? Suicide isn't a crime. No need for CID to be involved. For all practical purposes, Pollard was on his own. But the scenario had to be convincing—without suggesting any link between him and Beth.'

Anne drew her chair closer. 'Hence the play-acting over that letter.'

'Exactly.' I closed my eyes and tried to concentrate. 'I think—and this is only a guess—I think they were up against a problem. Stephen typed his correspondence. But . . . . a typed suicide note? Anyone could write that. Pollard had to avoid the slightest hint of suspicion.

Maybe that old handwritten envelope gave them the idea. Beth must have had it over a year—"waste not, want not"—without any thought of using it the way they did in the end. They couldn't hope to forge a whole letter. Far too risky. So they concocted the epistle that never was. Now you see it—now you don't. By saying she'd destroyed it, Beth fostered the illusion she and Pollard were on opposite sides.'

'They could have gotten away with it—if we hadn't turned up on Wednesday evening.'

'We had an advantage, but it didn't do us much good. Right up to this morning I believed Andrew Garland put that letter together. But Pollard made one big slip . . . and I remembered it too late. He said he searched the Priory from cellar to attic after Stephen's death. But Wright's body must have been in the cellar by then. Why didn't he mention it? He couldn't have missed it. If only I'd thought of that sooner, Ron might—'

'Ssh.' She kissed my eyelids softly. 'You know what he'd say. Don't fret—*boyo*.'

A young nurse crackled starchily to the foot of my bed. 'Mr Meynell should be resting now,' she said pointedly.

Anne rose to leave but I caught her hand. 'Don't go!' The last thing I wanted was to be left alone with my thoughts.

Beth talked. Thankfully I was not there to listen, but Inspector Young described how, once started, confession had poured from her as though every word were soothing ointment for the anguish of her seared body and soul.

Power . . . passion—the twin elements in the explosive compound which wreaked such havoc in Tongston that hot dry summer.

Pollard could never forget his former exalted rank in colonial force. Expansive days under African skies ha left him disgruntled. Tongstone Police House was poo exchange for a bungalow staffed by native boys. Lik Andrew Garland, he found the England of reality a variance with the idealized homeland of his dreams Disillusion drew the two men together. Pollard turned blind eye to the paramilitary activities in and around th Lodge—neglect which did not pass unnoticed by loca inhabitants and fellow-officers. Only later—when th Lodge was thoroughly examined—did the police dis cover his name on the list of active REAP members.

'*A member of a police force shall at all times abstai from any activity which is likely to interfere with th impartial discharge of his duties, or which is likely to giv rise to the impression among members of the public that may so interfere; and in particular a member of a polic force shall not take any active part in politics.'—Polic Regulation. 1965.*

At the same time, Pollard formed a relationship wit an ambitious woman. For years Beth had been growin apart from her husband. Stephen was content to farm hi acres and maintain Tongstone Priory as he had known since childhood—a peaceful home where he could relax write and entertain his small circle of friends. She grew increasingly bitter at his refusal to consider schemes fc exploiting its tourist potential.

In the sergeant she found a kindred spirit, but the matched ambitions were to drive them to desperat action. For Beth, the prospect of Stephen's blindnes was intolerable. He shared his unhappy secret with he s soon as he learned the specialist's prognosis. She vinced sympathy, but in reality thought only of the estrictions to be imposed on her by his condition after urgery. So she began to dream of the seeming impos-ible—freedom from her husband; control of the Priory.

Pollard too had dreams. Life in a stately home with a eautiful woman. Advancement in his career. A return o the status he had known before colonial independ-nce. But more obtrusive than those dreams was the ightmare of professional disgrace. Discovery of his dulterous relationship with Stephen Garland's wife had een a threat ever since the affair began. Now a new anger had arisen. Stephen, gathering material for his elevised lecture, had turned his attention to REAP. here was a grave risk that Andrew, jealous for the eputation of his cherished organization, might already ave compromised the sergeant with rash boasts about he quality and standing of REAP's membership.

Power . . . passion—and a slow fuse in the shape of ne discarded envelope, salvaged from Stephen's waste-asket and casually preserved in Beth's writing desk. Vith her annual vacation in prospect she had dreamed lly of receiving a letter in that envelope. A letter which ould tell that her fondest desire had been granted. ogic laughed at her fantasy. Only Stephen's death ould fulfil that wish.

Thus unimpassioned logic sowed the seed . . .

Stephen Garland would die as though by his own and—and Sergeant Pollard would investigate the agedy.

The suicide letter was written and posted in the morn-ig of Wednesday July 14.

At seven-thirty that evening Pollard called Beth's

hotel from his home and spoke to the receptionist as Stephen Garland. The first witness had been primed. Then he left the Police House, walked along the deserted railway, skirted the copse by the Lodge and reached the Priory unseen. The presence of Andrew Garland and Alex Howell was unexpected, but Pollard had the gift of patience. Howell left shortly after eight and Andrew fifteen minutes later. Five minutes more and Stephen was in his study, selecting a recording for his customary post-prandial relaxation. As soon as he was settled, deaf to the world about him because of the headphones, Pollard moved swiftly from his hiding place, collected the Colt Python from the gunroom using a key provided by Beth, loaded it with one bullet and—walking openly into the study—shot Stephen as he sat enthralled by Elgar's *Enigma Variations*.

But his plan had already faltered. Minutes ahead of us, Colin Wright was hurrying past the study window obviously alarmed by the sound of the shot. Pollard dropped the Python and raced back to the gunroom.

Opening the front door, Wright made straight for the study where the sight that greeted him cried *Murder*. Whether or not he had glimpsed Pollard through the study window we shall never know. With courage worthy of respect he snatched up the revolver and set off to search the house—unaware that the gun he carried was now empty. In contrast, Pollard had found and loaded a sporting rifle. Creeping silently from room to room, the two men hunted each other through the house.

Sounds of our arrival brought Wright hurrying to the study door. The noise of Andrew Garland's phone call covered our escape and by the time we reached the old uins, Pollard had found his quarry. Wright fell to the hot I imagined aimed at me.

Unaware of our visit, Pollard acted fast, dumping Vright's body in the cellar before returning to the study o create the illusion of Stephen's suicide. His final act efore leaving was to switch those records. His knowedge of music was slim. The Mahler was Beth's idea. tephen might have selected musical comedy for his vening's entertainment—hardly an appropriate valeiction.

Although he worked quickly, Pollard's carefully lanned schedule was ruined. He had to be back at the 'olice House before Constable Redgrave arrived to egin the regular round of their manor—a tour which vould bring them to the Priory and the discovery of tephen's body. In desperation he took the Landrover nd drove back along the railway to Furzeby Station vhere he hid it in the disused engine shed.

Later, when the two police officers searched the 'riory, Pollard took the leading role his rank demanded. And he made sure he alone entered the cellar.

For two days he remained ignorant of our part in the rama. Disposal of Wright's body was his most pressing roblem. He called Beth by phone but dared not risk isiting the Priory.

Then Andrew Garland stumbled on to the scene. Bent n vengeance for his brother's death . . . his suspicions f Beth aroused by our news of the letter, he determined o carry out his own investigation at the Priory. Fortified vith whisky and armed—as befitted a man hunting his rother's murderer—he dragged himself from room to oom. And at last, he shuffled to the top of the cellar teps, lost his footing—and tumbled into oblivion.

With the discovery of Wright's body, Pollard was no longer master of his fate. CID had taken over. The Landrover, concealed within yards of his home, could direct unwelcome attention in his direction. He chose a bad time to return it.

Constable Redgrave was no time-serving plodder. Involved with his community, he was aware of the subtle undercurrents of country life. What he did not know, he sensed. His eyes told him Pollard had ignored some highly-suspicious activity at the Lodge. Instinct whispered that his sergeant was indiscreetly involved with the lady of the Priory. Wright's body alerted him to the presence of a killer. Unofficial overtime, late on Friday night, brought the dubious satisfaction of seeing Pollard creep forth in the moonlight and head towards the abandoned railway. Redgrave's first thought—a midnight assignation—was quickly dispelled by the sound of a car's engine. Breathless, he topped the rise of the station approach to see the Landrover emerge from the old engine shed and lurch away down the track.

His call to CID at Brentwell brought a patrol car to the Priory. Understandably I was not told the true reason for its timely arrival.

Suspicion, now fixed on Pollard, extended to Beth when she called Brentwell Police on Saturday morning to ask about surveillance of the Priory. The Duty Sergeant realized she could be seeking confirmation that the house was not being watched. Ron's phone call, half an hour later, was no surprise.

As Pollard hurried along the old railway, his control was giving way. Too many things had gone wrong. Maybe he already sensed Redgrave's suspicions. He was armed with an unlicenced revolver treasured from his colonial days. By the time he reached the Priory he was jumpy. Ron's sudden challenge, coming from that darkened passage, proved too much . . .

THURSDAY JULY 22. Oven-hot on the hillside above Abertandy. Anne, Clare and I had followed the coffin from *BETHESDA*—the neat Calvinistic Methodist Chapel—up steep streets shadowed by a vast pit-tip to the marble-cluttered cemetery.

As the old pastor spoke his words of committal I stared down into the open grave.

RONALD LLEWELLYN METCALFE
Born 18th January 1931 . . .
Died 17th July 1976

Put that way, it didn't amount to much.

A spattering of dry earth hit the coffin and powdered the brass plate. I glanced up to see a woman in black casting more drought-parched soil into the grave.

'. . .*dust to dust* . . .'

On our way down the hill we overtook the Director stumping ponderously towards his chauffeur-driven limousine.

'Ah, Meynell. Hardly the time or place, perhaps, but I just wanted a word—'

'*Who's the woman?*'

'Woman?' He followed my gaze. 'Oh—*that* one. Gwyneth Metcalfe. The widow.'

I stared at the little group by the open grave. 'I didn't even know he was married.'

'Yes—well . . . sensitive area, I believe.' He opened a leather cigar-case. 'Didn't work out. Silly girl couldn't accept that the Department comes first.'

I turned to Anne. 'I didn't even know he was married,' I repeated huskily. It seemed terrible—to work alongside a man for years and not know that.

The Director set a match to his cigar. 'Mmm. Couple of children too, I believe. Or is it *three?* You didn't know? Well—why should you? They've been living apart for years. Quaint ideas about divorce. Rather touching in a way. Now—to business. There's another assignment—' He stopped and looked round to where we had halted, ten feet behind him.

'You go on,' I said. 'There's something I have to do.'

He shrugged. 'Don't be long. I'm dining with the PM.'

I turned and headed back up the hill, reaching out my left hand to Anne. My jacket slipped from my injured shoulder and Clare carefully hitched it back into place over the sling bandage.

The woman in black was talking to the pastor beside Ron's grave. As we passed her eyes met mine and she nodded. It was as though she already understood something I was only beginning to realize. Anne's grip tightened on my hand and in that moment I knew—some things could only be fully grasped if others were let go.

Beyond the cemetery we were on open hillside where sheep grazed shrivelled pasture. Five minutes later we reached the crest. Ahead, to the north, lay rolling moorland and distant mountains. Pausing, we looked back.

Below us the cemetery was deserted, except for a sexton slowly shovelling earth into the grave. At the foot of the hill the Director stood beside his car, staring up at us. He seemed to be beckoning.

Clare said, 'Gee, but he looks little from up here.'

With Anne's hand in mine we turned and walked on towards the far mountains.